Ryan Hunter

THIS GIRL IS MINE

A GROVER BEACH TEAM BOOK

GENRE: YA/CONTEMPORARY ROMANCE

This book is a work of fiction. Names, places, characters and incidents are either the product of the author's imagination or are used fictitiously. Any resemblance to actual people, living or dead, businesses, organizations, events or locales is entirely coincidental.

BOOKS BY ANNA KATMORE

Play With Me

Ryan Hunter

T is for...

Kiss With Cherry Flavor

*

Summer of my Secret Angel

*

Neverland

Pan's Revenge

To my dear readers!

A few months ago, I made the best decision ever. I hit the publish button for PLAY WITH ME. But in my wildest dreams, I didn't believe that so many of you would fall in love with Lisa and Ryan. I'm getting the loveliest emails from you every day, telling me thanks for writing such a sweet love story. Now, I think it's time to say THANKS to all of you for supporting me, encouraging me, and cheering me on to keep writing. Without you, RYAN HUNTER would have never been born. I hope you enjoyed this little POV switch and fell in love with Ryan once again!

From the heart,
Anna

Ryan Hunter

THIS GIRL IS MINE

ANNA

KATMORE

Dear
Alyssa

This will help you
in this Book
Tony and Lisa are
BF and GF But
Ryan Hunter like
her.

From

Alyssa

ANNA KATMORE

CHAPTER 1

I'D HAD MY fair share of girls in high school, that wasn't a secret. But I had never really been in love. Well, not with any of the ones I'd had, anyway.

And still, there was *her*. She climbed out of Mitchell's car, tossed her long brown hair over her shoulder, and adjusted the pink tee that was a snug fit and accentuated all the good stuff. The bright morning sun blinded her, and she squeezed her eyes to thin slits, which made the corners of her sweet mouth move up into something similar to her beautiful smile. And as always when my gaze got stuck on Lisa Matthews, I felt something slithery in my chest move into place.

She didn't look my way. Never had. And why would she? Her universe was rotating around my soccer buddy, Tony Mitchell. As long as I had known Tony, he'd always come in a double pack. He and Lisa were what some people at school called M&M. I hated that term. Hated how she stood on her tiptoes now and slung her arms around his neck. Hated how—

Dammit! Was she going to *kiss* him? My stomach hardened in a way that made me want to claw those muscles apart. But damn, I was a man. I wouldn't give away how tense I was. Or so I thought as I stood stiff as an ironing board and failed to tear my gaze away from the two of them.

They had never kissed. Lisa was in love with Tony, and I would bet my *Need for Speed* collection that he loved her back in a very odd, very secret way. But they *Had. Never. Kissed.* And that was good, because if they had, I might have gone over there now and rearranged my buddy's face so that not even his family would recognize him afterward.

"Relax, bro. It's just a peck on the cheek."

I turned to Justin, who'd sneaked up on me and slapped my shoulder, and I let out the familiar breath that I held every time Lisa got too close to Mitchell.

"Yeah, it better be. I'd hate to go *murder* on a good friend today." I grinned at Justin and did the ghetto handshake we'd been doing since we were out of primary school and became the cool kids who roamed the corridors of Grover Beach High.

Justin Andrews wasn't a member of the Bay Sharks, the school's soccer team, which I happened to be the captain of. He'd never cared for soccer but was actually a pro on his BMX bike. What he could do was amazing, but only for people who had a serious death wish. Jumping from bridges with his bike or balancing on picket fences earned him bruised bones and awesome black eyes nearly every weekend. Today he'd come to see his little brother off, who was only one year younger than us and actually played soccer on my team.

Justin jerked his chin to my left. "Are you going over there to say goodbye to the girl?"

"Why would I do that? We haven't even made it to the

hello yet."

"Dude, if they haven't become a couple in ten years, they probably never will be. It's about time to let her know about the other fish in the sea that's trying to get a bite of her." He scratched his chin. "If you won't do it, maybe I will. After all, you and that Mitchell guy are gone at soccer camp for five weeks."

I slung a chummy arm around his neck, pressing a little harder than necessary. In fact, if I'd been any less gentle, the boy would have been blue in the face in a minute. "You can try, dude. But you know not even the FBI would find your body then."

He punched me in the ribs so I let him go. But we were laughing so hard that some of the guys and their parents turned their heads our way. We didn't give a shit about them but bickered some more, until I heard a familiar voice shout my name.

My sister came over and caught me in a hug that was impossible to evade. "I have to go. Phil's waiting. Be careful, baby brother."

"Yeah, sure." I tried to fend Rachel off when she kissed my cheek. This was okay at home or anywhere people didn't know me. But in front of my soccer buddies this was just unacceptable. "Go away, Rach. And take care of Mom and Dad while I'm gone."

"I'm pretty sure they're old enough to take care of themselves, but I'll drop by for dinner once in a while if they feel alone or miss their pretty baby." She laughed and ruffled my hair. Then she headed back to the parking lot near the train station.

Some of the kids had already boarded the train and were waving goodbye from the open windows. As I picked up my duffel bag and walked toward my coach, I caught a glimpse of the last thing I wanted to see this morning. Mitchell and Lisa in a pose that pressed her perfect body flush to his. He leaned down those few inches that he was taller than her and whispered something into her ear that made her blush an adorable pink.

"Man, you're pitiful." Justin shoved me forward, and only then did I realize that I had actually stopped walking.

Gnashing my teeth and keeping my eyes glued to the much safer ground in front of me, I moved past Mitchell and the girl I'd been dreaming of since ninth grade.

"Hey, Hunter."

I knew I should just keep walking. I'd see Tony in a minute on the train, anyway. But the weaker part of me looked up just as Tony let go of my girl. "Hi, Mitchell," I said as my gaze went out of control and swept over Lisa, taking in every inch of the suntanned skin that her illegally short pants exposed. I acknowledged her and cracked a smile. "And Mitchell's groupie."

She didn't say *good morning* or *how are you doing* or even *get lost and don't ever talk to me again*, though the latter might have been written in her green eyes which always seemed to turn a demonic shade darker when she looked at me. I knew she wasn't my greatest fan. Not because she personally hated me, but because she blamed me for taking away her precious time with Tony. Mitchell had let that bit of information slip one day after she had all but growled at me for doubling the training time.

"See you, Mitchell," I said and walked away.

"Save me a seat in your compartment," Tony shouted after me.

I waved at him over my shoulder but didn't look back. "Sure thing." If it wasn't me and Justin doing something stupid, it was always me and the guys on the team hanging out. We were really close. Like *closer than family* close. And yet, none of them knew of my obsession with a girl that only had eyes for my best player. Yeah, sometimes you just had to accept the crap life threw at you and put a shit-eating grin on your face.

I climbed the two steps into the coach before turning around to bump fists with Justin. "Enjoy the sun in Santa Monica," he said. "I hear the girls down there are hot!"

"I'll check them out and let you know." Maybe. If I could get Lisa off my mind long enough to relax with another girl, something I hadn't done in quite a few months. If this madness was going to hang on any longer, my reputation would be in serious trouble soon. Unfortunately, I had a weird feeling that it was only going to get worse for me.

Justin pointed a finger at my face. "And you take care of Nick. If he comes back with one scratch on his skin, I'll hold you personally responsible."

"Yeah, right." I flipped him off, because we both knew that his little brother was...well, a little accident prone. Whatever happened during the next five weeks at our annual summer soccer camp, that kid would come back with a limb in a cast—no matter what. The question was just which limb it was going to be. Some of the guys on the team had a bet running. I had twenty bucks on any finger of his left hand, but Justin didn't have to know that.

I found Frederickson and Alex Winter in a four-seat compartment in the middle of the train. We waited until Tony joined us, then closed the opaque sliding doors and settled in for the three-hour ride. We had chips, we had root beer, and it was just us guys. I decided that the next five weeks were going to be one helluva good time for all of us. But then I sneaked a glance out the window and caught Lisa still standing at the platform, her arms folded around her middle, her face sad.

If that look had been because of me and not Mitchell, I would have felt a lot better.

The first three days at camp were hell. We played a serious schedule every day, and by the time we were let off, our legs were on fire. By then, we weren't up for anything other than grabbing some food and dropping onto our pillows. But we got used to the drill fast, and on day four, Mitchell, Winter,

Frederickson, and I thought it was okay to stretch the camp rules a little and sneak out after dark for some fun.

Santa Monica had a few very cool places for students to hang out. No alcohol in the place called "The Teen Spirit," but awesome music and some eye candy, too. It didn't take long for a bunch of girls to close in on our table like we were the light to their moth lives. Two of them each sported something black that could barely be called a dress, and the other three were plastered into skintight jeans and tops that left the navel exposed to our view.

"Hi, guys," one of them said, batting her lashes at me. Her eyes were a striking navy blue. I guessed that she was barely seventeen, still a year younger than me, probably a junior. "We usually know all the good-looking boys who come here. You must be visiting?"

Okay, she was a brave one, and not only because she dared to come here in heels that were longer than my middle finger and clearly gave her trouble walking. I wondered if she would have said that if she'd been facing us alone, without her lioness pack to back her up.

"We're playing soccer just outside the city," I told her. "Over the next few weeks, you might have time to get used to us coming here."

She smiled a wide welcome and hooked her brunette hair behind her ears, revealing pirate hoops for earrings. "Mind if we sit down?"

"Sure," I grabbed a seat from the vacant table behind me

and pulled it around so that she'd sit right next to me. I didn't know why. Maybe because Frederickson had made the most hopeful face when the girls came over, or maybe just because it was an old habit. Whichever it was, I regretted doing it the moment the other girls got chairs, too, and the pirate replica scooted so close that our legs touched under the table.

Gentlemen that we were, we paid for a round of sodas and made some casual conversation, but other than Frederickson, none of us guys seemed really impressed with the catch we'd made. The girl next to me, who had introduced herself as Sandy, ordered a mineral water and leaned in a little too close to say thank you. When I looked at her face, all I could think was that I'd prefer a girl who came clean and natural, without all the colorful cement on her face. I leaned back a few inches then widened the space between us to a solid foot. Not only was she painted like Picasso's first test subject, but she also seemed to have fallen into a pot of her mother's perfume, which stung my nose.

I'd stood next to Lisa a million times, and the floral scent of her shampoo and soap had never curled my toes.

Mitchell was having trouble warding off a strawberry blonde, who flashed braces in a flirtatious smile at him. It would have been interesting to know if he was avoiding her because of the same girl that was on my mind right now. We made it through one hour, but finally Tony and I shared a look that said, *Run, and run as fast as you can*.

To escape, we produced a lame ass excuse. That we

ANNA KATMORE

weren't allowed to stay out so late or we'd get thrown out of soccer camp, which wasn't exactly a lie, but also nothing that we were really bothered with.

"Will you come back this weekend?" Sandy asked and curled a strand of her hair around her forefinger. God, who had taught this girl to flirt? It was like she had watched the worst chick flicks ever and taken notes.

Okay, maybe she wasn't that bad, and a few months ago, I might even have encouraged her flirting, but tonight I wasn't in the mood. "Guess we will. But we'll probably bring our girlfriends, too, so this round won't happen again."

That made her back off, and I wasn't in the least sorry for pulling that shitty lie out of nowhere. I tapped Frederickson on the shoulder and interrupted his making out with a girl who had hair as red as his. "We're off, dude. Are you coming?"

He bit his lip, seriously deliberating. Then he detached himself from the girl he called Kelly and walked out the door with us.

"I've never been that happy to get away from a bunch of girls," Mitchell said as we climbed over the threaded wire fence back at camp.

"Why?" Frederickson mumbled. "The chicks were willing. What's your problem? Don't wanna get laid?"

Tony and I simultaneously smacked him upside the head. "I don't like it when a girl doesn't take no for an answer," I told him, then held the door to our dorm room open for the rest to slip inside. "And Sandy's hand on my thigh definitely hasn't heard the word *no* before."

We crawled into the bunk beds and turned off the light.

As I walked out to the training grounds the following morning, I knew at first sight that this was going to be a special day. A group of girls, all dressed in soccer jerseys and cleats, sat on the lush green lawn, apparently waiting for us. This was the first year that girls had come, too. We've heard that the school administration felt guilty for not sponsoring a girls' team at Grover Beach High, so they sent the girls along to soccer camp to make up for it.

Initially I'd thought that was a good idea. But when the coach told us to gather into co-ed teams, I was a little skeptical. We'd never played with girls before. They were fragile and breakable and definitely shouldn't have been out on the field with us rowdy guys.

"Hi, Hunter," two girls from my chemistry class greeted me.

"Hi, McNeal. Summers," I said without stopping to talk to the two blondes. Chloe Summers was a capable player from what I'd seen the past three days on the other field, and Brinna McNeal seemed glued to her heel, no matter what.

For the sake of everyone's bones, the guys and I toned it down a little as we started the first match. Maybe this was foolish of us, because before the first half was over, Chloe had fouled me three times, and I don't mean gentle, womanly fouls. Twice she rammed into me at full speed and the last time she'd hooked her right leg around my ankle so that I went sailing a

ANNA KATMORE

couple yards before I bellyflopped onto the grass.

I took a moment to pump air into my lungs again then climbed to my feet and headed toward her. Since she almost matched my six-foot-two, I could easily press my brow to hers and growl in her face. "Ah, you're such a *lady*, Summers."

"Sorry, did I hurt your feelings?" she countered with a grin that sat custom-made for trouble on her lips. "Can we continue with the game now, or do you need a minute to catch your breath, Hunter?"

I'd known that girl my whole life, since she only lived three streets away from me, and she'd never interested me one bit. But her aggressive style left an impression that day, and after two weeks of occasionally playing with the girls, I decided to chew through a topic with the guys on my team.

The Teen Spirit was the place where we would talk tonight. We hadn't gone there since our first night out, and I wondered if Sandy and her lionesses would be around again. Guilty of the stupid lie about our girlfriends, I had a queasy feeling as we walked through the door. The feeling grew when we spotted the lionesses hanging out by the bar.

Very much to Frederickson's dismay, we chose a table at the far end of the room. The place was packed on this Saturday night, and so we lost those junior chicks easily enough.

"I was thinking," I started, only to be immediately interrupted by Alex.

"Hear, hear!"

"Shut up, Winter!" I punched him on the shoulder. "So,

anyway, I was saying, what do you guys think about a co-ed team back home?"

All seven of my players leaned forward to rest their arms on the table. *"What?"*

"Not all the time, don't panic! But you saw that playing with them isn't half bad. I was thinking we could sort of recruit the best of them and then split our training time. Half time with and half time without the chicks."

"If they agree, anyway," Tony pointed out.

"I saw Chloe Summers and her friends near the entrance when we came in. If you're cool with the idea, I'll get them, and we can discuss this together."

There was a collective silence. Slowly, grins began to grow on their faces. "Sounds like a plan to me. I'm in," Frederickson said.

I knew he would be swayed easily because, out of all of us, he seemed to have the most fun with the girls.

Mitchell pulled a skeptical face. "I don't know about this. I mean, they wouldn't be playing the big games with us, anyway, so why sacrifice training time?"

"Well the girls don't have a team at school and even though we wouldn't play important games with them, we could play some friendly matches. I know Hamilton High has a co-ed team, too, and unless I'm very much mistaken, so do the Riverfalls Rabid Wolves. They're two teams we could invite for a game once in a while. It just seems fair to give the girls a chance to play, too." Then I laughed and slapped him on the shoulder. "If it helps, you can ask your girlfriend to join the team as well."

"Who? *Liz?*" He made a baffled face. "She'd rather touch a leper than a soccer ball. And she's not my girlfriend."

"Yeah, right." I was teasing him, but to hear the truth out of my friend's mouth felt unspeakably good. "So, do we ask the girls now or not?"

The guys agreed as one. I got to my feet and headed over to the bar where I had last glimpsed Chloe, Brinna, and three other girls from our school. Tough luck—right next to them stood Sandy and the junior chicks. Sandy saw me walking closer, and the fact that I was alone seemed to make her happy. Her smile moved into place, and she said *hi* to me.

"Hey, Sandy."

"No girlfriend again?" It sounded like a mix of accusation for the lie I had told her and delight over finding me still single.

I didn't want to give her false hope, and more importantly, I didn't want to spend the next hour fending her off again, so I grabbed the first familiar girl I saw and pulled her to my side. "Sorry to disappoint you," I told a baffled Sandy. "But I just came over to get my girl." I tilted my head to see who my girl actually was and found myself nose to nose with Chloe. She lifted a delicate brow at me but was cool enough to handle the moment. "You ready to come back to the table with me, hun?" I said through a grin.

Chloe caused me a second of panic, but then she played along. "Of course, baby. Let me just tell the girls that we're moving. And that you agreed to pay for a round."

I gritted my teeth behind tight lips, but the rescue was worth it. With my arm still around Chloe, I walked her over to our table in the back, knowing that Sandy would stare after us with those disappointed navy blues.

Chloe played her part a little too well. She was overdoing it when she wrapped her arm around my waist and shoved her hand into the back pocket of my jeans.

"Hands out of there, Summers," I growled, but kept her tucked to my side.

"Why? You have a sexy ass, Hunter." She laughed and pinched my butt cheek before moving her hand out of my pocket and up to safer grounds.

The guys had already found chairs for the ladies, and I was more than happy when I could let go of Chloe and slump back into my seat.

"Wow, this looks like you've been expecting us," she said as they all sat down. "What's up?"

"There's something we want to discuss with you," I replied.

"Really? And here I thought you only wanted to use one girl to escape another."

I grimaced. "Yeah...thanks for that." Then I ordered sodas for all of us, and we told the girls what we had in mind.

All of them were intrigued by the idea, especially since they didn't have a girls' team back in Grover Beach. The most soccer they got was in gym class, and only when the teacher was

ANNA KATMORE

having a good day.

"I know of a few girls at school who would love to be on a team," Brinna said. "If you don't mind that they aren't all going to be seniors next year."

"It's actually only Sasha, Tyler, and myself who are going to be seniors on our team," I pointed out. "So you don't have to worry."

"Cool. I can text a few girls back home and we can all meet up when we're back. How many girls do you need for the co-ed team?"

"I don't know. Eight to ten would be good. If there are more who want to join, we'll have to hold tryouts."

The evening wore on a few more hours, before we finally left the bar together.

"Everybody grab a girl," Alex said over his shoulder with a grin as we passed Sandy and her lionesses by the bar.

I wanted to tuck Chloe under my arm again, because she was walking next to me, but the blonde gave me a grim look. "Take Brinna," she snapped, then she hooked her arm through Tony's and batted her lashes at him. "I want to be *his* girlfriend for the walk out."

Mitchell raked a hand through his blond hair and let loose a shit-eating grin. "Sorry, Hunter."

He didn't have to be. Brinna was as good a match as anyone, and I released her as soon as the door had fallen shut behind us. However, Chloe clung to Mitchell's arm the entire way home. Then I got an update from Frederickson on the flirting that had apparently been going on all evening, and which I had completely missed.

Summers and Mitchell? Now, why did that thought make me grin to myself?

Back at camp, I threw a quarter in the soda machine in the hall, just to get a chance to see how Tony and Chloe would part tonight. Knowing Chloe, I was sure she'd go for a kiss, and if she did, this could finally be my chance with Lisa. If Tony was taken, she'd realize sooner or later that he wasn't the only boy in the world.

I took a swig of Coke, watching them from the corner of my eye. To my total frustration, they didn't kiss. They didn't even talk about meeting the next morning at soccer training. All they said was "Good night," and Chloe added, "Sleep tight, Anthony."

Tony waited for me when she was gone and, together, we climbed the steps to the boys' dorm. I didn't touch on the topic, and neither did he.

CHAPTER 2

CHLOE SUMMERS WAS the female equivalent of me. Heading from one fling into the next and enjoying uncomplicated relationships that lasted about two to three weeks maximum and left us free of any ties. I was perfectly aware of the terms *playboy* or *school hottie* that most of the girls used in combination with my name. While *I* didn't want to be bound to anyone because the girl I wanted walked in front of me every day, totally unaware of how I felt, I didn't understand what kept Chloe from having a deep and meaningful relationship.

She'd flittered through half the guys at soccer camp by the time we evacuated our dorms when the five weeks were up, and she'd certainly made a name for herself because of that. There were only a few of us who were immune to her flirting, and Tony Mitchell definitely didn't fall into that group. It would be a lie to say I didn't hope they would hook up, even though he was my friend and deserved better. But she'd been the first girl in like forever that he seemed to be interested in—apart from Lisa—and I couldn't help getting my hopes high whenever I saw the two of them together. I would never hit on any friend's girl. But if Tony was with someone else, he couldn't claim Lisa

Matthews as his own any longer.

On the train it was the four of us again: Alex, Frederickson, Tony, and me. We had all tanned nicely from playing in the sun and were fooling around like cocky jocks, bragging about how the girls would be at our feet when we got back. But the truth was, only Frederickson really meant it, because I...well, I had stopped plucking girls from every corner of the school's corridors some serious time ago. And Tony was texting like mad with Lisa, while Alex Winter had finally come out with why he had been so low-key around the fairer sex during the past five weeks. There was a girl on his mind, too. A special one. And he intended to get her to go out with him eventually, even though she'd rebuffed him twice before the last school year ended. Her name was Simone, and I thought I remembered her from the parties I sometimes threw. Parties at which I'd always hoped to see Lisa walking through my front door, but as it was, Tony had never passed my invitations on to her. He said she was too nice to be dragged into a hellhole like my house on a Saturday night, but I was sure he was just scared someone else would hit on her and she might like it.

I glanced at my friend who had just punched out another text message. He was surely telling Lisa that we'd be home in about two hours, and she was probably sitting in her room, biting her nails because she couldn't wait to see him again.

"Are you two making out over the phone or what?" I mocked and kicked his tennis shoe with the toe of mine.

Tony glanced up with this innocent *What?* look in his

eyes.

"You've sent Lisa over twenty messages in the past half hour," Alex said, backing me up with a sneer. "What's so urgent that it can't wait until we're home?"

"Nothing." Tony cleared his throat and tucked the cell into his pocket. "I was just giving her an update about the past few days. Because Hunter wants to meet with the others about this co-ed thing right when we get back, she'll be in a terrible mood since I can't hang out right away."

"Dude, give it a break. Just make her come along with you. I don't see why you're being so complicated," I said. But the truth was, I was jealous, and more than just a little bit. I wished I could text back and forth with Lisa on the way home, have her all euphoric to see me again, and wrap her up in a tight hug, which Tony would doubtlessly do when he walked over to her house in a little while.

"She won't come. She hates soccer, and when I mention your name, her face usually turns into a grimace." Tony smirked. "No offense, Hunter."

"None taken," I muttered and turned to stare out the window. Lisa was probably the only girl in the universe that was resistant to my charm. Goddammit! But then again, she hadn't seen much of it so far. Since the girls of friends were a no-go for me, it made me tone down the flirt-factor automatically. It could all change with Chloe, though. A bubbly spark of hope lit in my chest. It made me feel stupid, and I struggled to get that feeling under control. I glanced sideways at Tony. "What about the

Summers chick?"

"What about her?"

"You two hung out a lot at camp."

His lips became a thin line. "Yeah. So what?"

Heck, we hadn't talked about her in all this time we were at camp, and now that I thought of it, it was because whenever someone mentioned Chloe's name, Mitchell changed the subject. "So, is there something going on between the two of you?"

"Why do you want to know?"

"Why don't you want to answer?"

Alex bumped his shoulder into Tony's. "Because this dude is in love, and it's not with Matthews."

Tony shoved him back. "Knock it off. I'm not in love with anyone."

"Then why are you so touchy all of a sudden?" Alex asked.

"And so defensive," I added.

"I'm not. You're just idiots."

Okay, we couldn't contradict that, but Tony's secretive love life was interesting me more and more. And then it hit me like a hammer on the head. "It's because of her!"

He quirked his brows at me. "Huh?"

"It's Chloe! Not me. She's the reason you don't want to bring Matthews along. You don't want the girls to meet, that's it!" Heck, I almost sneered at my friend because of my ingenuity.

And suddenly something weird happened, which none of

us guys could have predicted. Anthony Mitchell blushed a pretty, girly pink.

"Oh my fucking God!" I slapped my brow. "So you have something running with the Summers chick. And you're scared to tell little Lisa."

Tony raked a nervous hand through his hair. "She won't understand," he whined. It didn't help that at that moment another text from Lisa came in.

I knew it was an asshole move, but this time I couldn't resist. As soon as he fished the phone out of his pocket, I grabbed it and opened the text. Tony jumped at me, but I held it out of his reach and wrestled myself free.

"We can do whatever you want. Go for a swim? We haven't done that all summer. But then, you were *gone* all summer, you rascal," I read out loud, and the other two repeated, "*You rascal!*" in the most girly way one had ever heard. We laughed our asses off.

"Give it back. You're such an infantile, Hunter."

"*Infantile!*" we repeated and stuck our heads together like the three Stooges, already holding our stomachs from laughing. I was too weak to withstand Tony's attacks, so I let him have his phone back. God knew what he texted Lisa then. Likely, that he was trapped in a train compartment with the kindergarten of Grover Beach.

When the train stopped at our station, we grabbed our bags and jumped off the coach into the warm Friday afternoon sun. I stretched my back and cracked my neck, which had gone tiff during the ride. Then I scanned the place for a delicate brunette with apple-green eyes. She hadn't come, not even to pick up her best friend and childhood love. Not seeing Lisa for half of the summer and staying sane had been a challenge. Not seeing her *now* was torture.

But school was only three weeks away. I would be a man and bear it with a grin. Or so I told myself.

The guys and I bumped fists and shouted goodbyes to several other friends we'd made at camp. Then we fanned out to find our rides home. My dad would pick me up today, but before I found him, I ran into my friend Justin. He had a broken little brother by his side. Well, not everything of Nick Andrews was broken. Only his right wrist, which didn't bring me any money, but it made me feel bad for him. It had happened only three days ago, up until which point we'd all wondered if he'd make it home sound for once. No such luck for the kid.

Justin wore a grim expression, but before he could say anything I cut him short. "Dude, I wasn't even near him when it happened. He slipped in the shower. How could I have prevented that from happening, huh?"

He considered that for a second, then a grin curved his thin lips, and we went through our handshake ritual which ended with a fist-pound on each other's shoulder. "What's cracking?" he asked as he and Nick walked with me to the parking lot. Then he leaned in closer, so that only I could hear his taunt. "Did a nice babe come along and blast the Matthews girl out of your head?"

I grinned back. "Did you run a truck over your sacred BMX bike?"

"Nah," we said simultaneously and laughed. Then I slapped his little brother on the shoulder and told him, "See you at Charlie's in a bit."

My dad was waiting by our black Ford Chrysler. I gave him a brief one-armed hug, dumped my bag in the trunk, and climbed into the passenger seat. Though this year at camp had been epic, it was nice to be going home at last.

Mom must have been waiting like a lynx behind the door, because the moment I opened it, she caught me in a bear hug that knocked the breath out of my lungs.

"Mom," I croaked, but hugged her back and laughed. "Mom, let go. You're hurting me."

"Yeah, she missed you an awful lot," my dad told me as he squeezed through between the doorjamb and my mom and me.

"Five weeks. You have no idea," Mom exclaimed, then she stroked my cheek and kissed the other. "This house is way too empty with both kids gone."

Ever since my sister ran off at age twenty—okay, she didn't run off but moved to San Luis—I had become the sole center of my mom's affection. While Rachel had quit college to marry the owner of a bar, I was the good kid who still lived at home and intended to go into my father's business one day. He had a veterinary practice attached to our house and let me sneak in from time to time. I liked animals, and helping him treat the furry patients was cool.

When I made it out of my mom's possessive embrace, I emptied my duffel bag into the wash and rushed upstairs to shower off the smell of a long journey. With a towel loosely wrapped around my hips, I shaved, put on some *Axe Temptation*, and rubbed my dark hair dry. From my closet, I grabbed a white muscle shirt and baggy pants then shoved my feet into black skater shoes. Next to my bed stood my graffiti-style skateboard. I stared at it for a few moments then decided to leave my car in the garage for one more day and use this ride instead.

Mom's eyes widened when I came down the stairs with the board clutched under my arm. "Are you going out again? You've barely had time to say hello. And you didn't tell me how camp was."

"Yeah. I have a meeting with the guys from the team in"—I glanced at my watch—"fifteen minutes."

"Will you be back for dinner? I was going to make a seafood platter tonight."

My mouth spread into a huge grin. She knew I loved fish and shrimp prepared in all different ways and she usually prepared this for special occasions. Like when her beloved son came back from camp after five long weeks. There was only one thing to say to this. "I love you too, Mom." I kissed her on the cheek. "I won't be long. Just a couple hours, I promise. Then I'll tell you all about camp at dinner."

The kiss was my ticket to go. She could never deny me

anything when I was the sweet boy who wasn't ashamed of telling his mom he loved her.

Outside, I dropped the skateboard to the asphalt and headed to Charlie's Café.

As I stepped off my board just in front of the low fence, I recognized some of the kids who had gathered around a few tables in the shadowy garden area. The place buzzed with activity this Friday afternoon.

I left my skateboard by the entrance with a couple others and headed toward the group to take a seat at one end of the table. Brinna was right, there were quite a few girls interested in playing soccer. I hadn't expected this craze.

When Charlie came to take my order, I asked for a lemon juice and something to write with. A few minutes later, the tall, prematurely balding man brought me two white sheets of paper and a pen with my drink.

Tony wasn't there yet, so a tiny flicker of hope remained that he'd bring Lisa after all. I took a sip of my juice and glanced over at Chloe in this white dress that looked like it was painted on her skin. Then again, it probably wasn't such a good idea to introduce the girls today.

"All right," I said to get everyone's attention after I'd put my glass down. "It's cool that so many of you came today. But since we can't take on more than ten players, we'll have to find a way to make a choice. Usually, it's a tryout for the guys, so I was thinking of arranging one for tomorrow morning. Does anyone have a problem with that?"

There was some headshaking and mumbling that tomorrow was fine.

"Great. I'll put each of your names down on the list then, and if you know of anyone else who'd like to play with the Bay Sharks, tell them to be at the soccer field around ten."

I knew most of the girls here because they were either in my classes or I'd dated them once or twice in the past. When I was done with the list and lifted my head, my heart knocked seriously hard against my ribcage. Tony had just walked up to us, and with him was the most beautiful girl in the world.

Holy Jesus, how much I had missed the sight of her this summer! As always, her shiny green eyes caught my attention first. Looking at them reminded me of spring leaves. Lisa's beautiful hair was tied in a high ponytail and only a few strands slipped out in the front, framing her heart-shaped face.

The pink T-shirt she wore today was my favorite, because it fit her like a second skin. From beneath the collar, two neon green straps ran up and around her neck to tie in the back. A bikini I guessed, remembering the text message I'd read on Tony's phone earlier. She was up for a swim. And as I looked at her pretty, naked legs, I decided a swim was just what I needed to cool off. I pulled my cap a little lower over my forehead, tearing my eyes off my personal sunshine, and cleared my throat, which had gone from okay to dry-as-a-bone within moments.

They hadn't even made it to our table when Chloe rose from her seat. "You're late, Anthony. I almost thought you wouldn't come."

I found it hilarious how she was the only person I knew who ever called him Anthony, but he seemed to like it. When she walked to Tony and kissed his left cheek, all the hilariousness was blown out of the situation, and I found myself holding my breath. Alex and Frederickson seemed as stunned as Lisa and I obviously were. The scene went from bad to worse when Tony placed his hands on Chloe's hips and let her kiss his other cheek.

Right now I wished I had the guts to stand up and wrap Lisa in a tender hug, and not for my personal pleasure, but because she looked like she had been run over by a bus.

"Mixed soccer teams, huh?" she growled at Mitchell then took a seat next to him, which meant she was also sitting directly opposite Chloe.

The least I could do was tease her a little and cheer her up. "The tryouts are tomorrow, Matthews. I can put you on the list, if you're interested." She didn't seem particularly happy about my joke, which wasn't really a joke anyway, but an attempt to get her on a team where I could play with her twice a week and have a reason to touch her. But she sent a surprised look in my direction. Maybe because this was the most I had said to her in one breath in all the time I had known her. I'd always found it easier to resist her when I didn't have to talk to her.

"Liz and soccer?" Tony laughed. "You might as well try to get an elephant to dance the tango. Right, Liz?"

Oh shit. Could he be any more tactless? I'd never heard

him talk to Lisa in this mean way. When she turned her head to him, her eyes held a great lot of hurt. But it seemed I was the only one to notice.

And then the unthinkable happened. Chloe opened her mouth, and I knew nothing nice would come out. "The elephant part hits home."

There it was. Short, biting, and so Chloe-like. She definitely felt threatened by Lisa, or she wouldn't have had to revert to bitchiness to carve out her territory, which, in this instance, was Tony. Somewhere in the back of my head, I was impressed. Chloe really looked like she felt a thing or two for this boy.

And *this boy* had just epically failed the friend test. He didn't say one word when Summers insulted Lisa, and that—hooking up with Chloe or not—was totally intolerable. I wondered what Lisa was going to do.

"I tried puking up my meals in ninth grade, but that seems to be more your thing than mine," was her retort. Obviously, that girl wasn't as shy and silent as she made everyone believe.

I laughed, but apparently I was the only one who dared to. Everyone else was shocked into silence, trying to stay out of the line of fire.

"Did you just insult me?"

Yes, Summers, she did! Of course, this was a first for my female equivalent. She and I weren't used to being bested by anyone. I was pretty sure that hurt her on a level she would never let on.

Lisa seemed more than relieved when Tony got a text message and asked her if she'd like to stay or walk back home with him. I'd never seen anyone knock back an almost-full glass of soda as fast as Lisa did while she rose from her chair.

"Nope, I'm ready," she told him.

Tony shook his head at her, then he grimaced and shrugged in my direction.

"See you tomorrow, Anthony," Chloe called out after him.

With her chin low and her gaze fixed on the ground, Lisa gritted her teeth in a way that made me fear for her molars. I didn't want to be in her shoes right now. But then, it had been hard enough to be in *my* shoes the past few years whenever she was around. Maybe things were finally playing out to my advantage, sad as it made me to see her so crushed.

When she walked past me, I suddenly realized if I didn't act now, I might not get another chance. The least I could do was get her to come to the tryouts. Maybe if I could show her that soccer wasn't all bad, she'd be on my team. And pretty clear visuals of how I'd get closer to her were already playing in my mind.

In a mad lack of self-control, I almost reached out to grab her hand and make her stop. She couldn't walk away from me just yet. But I pulled myself together and kept my fingers laced over my stomach when I asked her, "How about it, Matthews? Will you try out for the team or not?"

She stopped dead and looked at me, seriously surprised. "I—"

"You shouldn't tease her. She's just not made for soccer," Tony said, cutting her off. He tried to push her on, away from me.

Oh, how I wanted to kick his ass for that.

I don't know what really swayed her at that moment, whether it was just the wish to spend more time with Tony, or if it had to do with Chloe's snorting laughter. But when she turned around to Mitchell and told him, "Know what? I think I'll just give it a shot," I had to really struggle to keep my stupid grin under control.

Tony gave her a dubious look. "You're shitting me."

Damn. She wouldn't dare change her mind, would she? But the look she threw Tony said *What do you wanna bet, buddy?* And it was obvious she'd bite his head off if he said just one more stupid word.

"Cool, so you're on the list." Now I couldn't help but smile. Also because, with her standing right in front of me, I could enjoy her beautiful view without seeming like a peeping Tom. The little strip of bare skin flashing out between her tee and shorts was an illegal temptation. "We meet at ten on the field," I murmured.

"I'll be there."

This held the seal of a promise. And I'd nail her to it.

Once more, her deliciously long legs dragged my gaze down. I wanted to touch them—*Lord, kill me now.* I drank in every inch of her exposed skin, from her thighs over the little bruise on her left knee, to her bare feet in those light blue flip-flops. I swallowed, forcing my glance back up to her face. We looked at each other for a silent second, which gave me a strange feeling of goose bumps at the back of my neck, like she knew I was seizing her with my eyes—and like she enjoyed it.

"Bring shoes," I told her and winked in a way she'd probably never seen from me.

Her lips parted very slightly. Just looking at them made me want to kiss her senseless. But I never got to hear whatever she'd contemplated saying, because Mitchell made her move.

When they were gone, I caught Alex staring at me, and it got on my nerves in the span of a millisecond. "What?" I mouthed at him.

Alex smirked and shook his head with backup from Frederickson, who did the same. I flipped them the bird, covering the gesture by dragging my cap a little deeper still. But a grin was sneaking to my lips, and I could do nothing to stop it.

CHAPTER 3

DINNER WITH MOM was exhausting. She knocked a hole in my head with her questions, and I struggled to enjoy my seafood between answering them. Right then, I decided I really needed to call her more often when I was gone for an extended period of time.

After dinner I got a text message from Mitchell asking me to meet him outside my house in twenty minutes. There was nothing else I had planned for the evening, so hanging out with him was cool. I asked him in when I opened the door a bit later, but he made a face and said he'd rather walk.

Walk? The guy who came to my house three times a week to play video games and who inhaled tons of cheese crackers every time? Who was the reason my mom now kept a supply especially for him? He shrugged off my invitation and just nodded in the direction of the old playground a few streets up. Something was off.

I nodded and started walking alongside him, tucking my hands deep into my pockets. "What's up, Mitchell?"

It took him a few moments to answer. "I'm totally screwed, man."

I cocked a brow at him. Tony cut me a glance, but then he

40   ANNA KATMORE

focused on the pavement again, dragging out a deep sigh. "I need your help with Lisa."

Ah heck, no! *Don't talk to me about her.* Giving another guy advice on how to make it right with the girl *I* wanted ranked seriously low on my wish-to-do list. Yet here I was, still biting my lower lip and answering, "What can I do?"

"I want her on the team."

I almost stopped walking. Okay, this was something I definitely wanted, too. "She said she'll come to the tryouts tomorrow. That's a start, isn't it?"

"Yes, she'll come. But you haven't seen her handle a soccer ball yet. I swear she'd rather burn it than touch it."

"That's just because she hates you playing all the time when you should be spending time with her instead." I winced. Why the hell did I say that?

Tony was distracted with kicking a stone in front of him, so he didn't notice my grimace. "Maybe. But she won't stand a chance at the tryouts tomorrow."

Aha. He was worried about her failing. He shouldn't be. Heck, I had been waiting too long for her to be on my team to care about her skills now. Whatever Lisa was going to do tomorrow, I'd make sure she was a member of the Grover Beach Bay Sharks at the end of the day.

But then I started to wonder. "Why do you want her on the team, anyway?"

We reached the playground where Rachel and I used to play every day when we were children, and while I took a seat on the swing, Mitchell sat on the slide, resting his elbows on his knees, staking me with a meaningful look. "You were right today. I'm kind of dating Chloe Summers."

Excuse me if I get up and do a stupid victory dance right now. I cleared my throat, kept my expression even, and said, "That's cool."

"I just don't know how to break it to Liz. She was pissed earlier because of a few things I did...or apparently didn't do. I don't want to hurt her, but I know it will be horrible for her if she finds out that I'm seeing another girl."

"Yep, you're going to break the girl. That's a given." *But don't you worry, I'll be there to make her feel better.* "So having her on the team helps you how?"

"Liz really hates Chloe. And that after only twenty minutes together. I'm hoping for them to get to know each other better. Maybe they'll become friends." Tony leaned back on the metal slide, crossed his arms behind his head, and gazed up at the already dark sky. "I don't want to lose Lisa just because I have a girlfriend now."

I didn't know what to say other than, "Tough situation." And it sure was for everyone. Didn't he see that I was the wrong person to be giving relationship advice when it came to that girl? It would be so easy to talk Mitchell into something that would drive a wedge between him and Lisa. But I liked Mitchell, and once again, I put my own needs aside and said what he needed to hear from a good friend.

"Are you sure you're doing the right thing, Mitchell? I

mean, Lisa Matthews is madly in love with you. Just the way every guy would probably wish for. She's nice, she's pretty, she's cool, and she's fun. That's everything I always hear from you." I heaved a deep sigh and swung a few times back and forth, seriously wishing I didn't have to say this. "What in the world is keeping you from hooking up with her?"

Tony sat up again, legs crossed. "I don't know." He sounded every bit sincere. "You know how much I like her. But I just can't see us being together in a way like I want to be with Chloe. Not that I don't find Lisa attractive, that's not it. Heck, she's probably the prettiest girl in town."

She sure was. I got more and more confused as he continued.

"But I already know her. Like every little thing about her. She's been my best friend since forever and I love hanging out with her. But Chloe..."

Oh boy, there was that devoted sigh that had gotten many men before him into trouble.

"She's so different. She's wild and tells me what she wants. It doesn't even bother her that she's a few months older than me and going to be a senior."

The chains of the swing rattled when I got to my feet and walked to a tree, leaning one shoulder against it, folding my arms over my chest. "You do realize that she might have said the same thing to all the other guys she was with in the past? And by 'with' I mean for a couple of weeks, if we stretch it."

"She told me it's different this time. That she hasn't felt

this for any other guy before."

Hah! I wanted to laugh about that, but it was late and dark and we were on a silent playground, so it would have made me sound like a mad serial killer. Besides, I wouldn't laugh at a friend.

"I think I want us to be official," Tony confessed.

I rubbed my hands over my face, feeling the need to drag Tony under a cold shower to open his eyes. "Look, I don't want to sound like the older brother now." Mostly because I always hated when Rachel did that shit with me. "But you should really think about it again. You and Chloe...well, you don't have a future together. She's not the type to go for a relationship. She's like—"

"You?"

"Yeah, thanks," I muttered. "But that's probably what it is. That girl has a record where guys are concerned. You're interesting to her now, but she'll dump you before you can put your pants back on."

"That won't happen. She really likes me."

Damn, he wouldn't listen. How very frustrating. I straightened, and my voice became cold. "You plan on sleeping with her any time soon?"

Tony pressed his lips together and shrugged one shoulder.

"Fine. We'll talk again then. But be prepared for the possibility that by the time you've messed with someone else, Lisa might not be there waiting for you to return to her."

"Liz and I becoming a couple, that's not going to happen.

I don't need her to wait for me. I just don't want to lose my friend."

"With the way she feels about you, that just might happen, Mitchell."

"I just need some time to tell her. So I want you and the guys to shut up about me and Chloe, until I get the chance to come clean."

I chuckled. "Just don't say I didn't warn you."

And then it became clear to me that I might destroy what little chance had just been dangling in front of my face if I said anything more. I didn't intend to give it up when Tony was so set on the course he was currently taking with Chloe. However, there was one thing I needed to get straight. The bark of the tree rubbed against my back when I pressed a little harder against the trunk. "You want Chloe? Take her. I'll keep my mouth shut. You want Matthews on the team? Consider her a member. But only under one condition."

"And that would be what?"

"As part of my team, everyone sees her as that, and no longer as your sacred little girlfriend." I paused to let that first bit sink in before I went on. "She plays soccer, she comes to my parties. You don't stop her. And whatever happens there—if guys hit on her—you keep it together, man."

Seconds passed, and Tony remained silent.

"I just don't want any rivalries on our team," I added. "Are we clear?"

Mouth still shut, Tony stood and slowly walked toward the

exit of the playground. He didn't turn around when he told me, "Deal."

I lay awake for half of the night, wondering if I should have tried harder to talk sense into my friend. He was going to fall flat on his face, and the jerk just didn't want to see it. If it was only about Chloe and him, I wouldn't have thought about it twice but instead let Mitchell head into the adventure and come out of it a wiser man.

However, I knew what was going to happen. I hated to think of Lisa getting hurt in the game and my friend flushing the chance that I had always wanted—and which he'd had his entire life—down the gutter.

But it was not my job to change the world. And after so many years of having a crush on Lisa, it was time to think about myself for once. Well, about myself and *her*. She'd be in my house tomorrow night as part of my team. After-match parties were customary, and heck, I'd make sure to throw one for the new team members after the tryouts. I punched a short invitation into my phone and sent the text off to a group of sixty people. They would spread the word. My mom was on the texting list, too, just in case I forgot to tell her about the party in the morning. I never had to worry about running late to stock the fridge. Drinks and snacks were always there, and some of the kids would bring beer and wine coolers, anyway. But the best thing was, tomorrow, the girl of my dreams would be there. Sometime after midnight I fell asleep with a grin on my face.

The next morning, I went through my usual routine of showering, shaving, and getting dressed, all with music thundering from the speakers in my room. Currently, it was P!nk and Nate Ruess asking for a reason. I liked the song, mostly because it was the ringtone of Lisa's cell phone, and listening to it reminded me of her.

I tugged the white soccer shorts up over my hips, sat down on the corner of my bed, and tied my shoes. The cleats went into my backpack to wear later on the field. I grabbed a fresh jersey and pulled it over my head. Over the lamp on my desk hung my Indians cap. It was my favorite and the one I wore most of the time at school, but as I was about to put it on this morning, I looked at myself in the large mirror attached to the door. My hair was still wet from the shower and all over the place. I knew that this chaotic look usually made girls go stupid. It was worth a try with Lisa. Back in the bathroom, I pressed a tiny bit of gel into my palm, just enough to fix the style without making it look sticky or coated.

The car keys jingled in my hand as I headed downstairs. From the dining room drifted noise, and I guessed my mother was in there. "Mom!" I shouted over my shoulder, already late. "You got the text?"

"Yes, darling!" she answered. "Your dad and I got an invitation to Mary Fisher's birthday celebration. We won't be home tonight!"

"Yesss," I hissed and punched my fist in the air. Parties were so much better when I had the run of the house. "I'm off to soccer. Laters!"

In our double garage, my Audi A3 was dwarfed by my dad's Chrysler, but I couldn't wait to get behind the wheel of my baby painted a shiny, nightfall silver. It had been a present from my parents for my eighteenth birthday, shortly before soccer camp. And with my own savings, I had turned the brand-new car into a real attention-catcher, with twenty-inch tires on specially designed aluminum rims, an epically mean-looking front, and the body slammed to the ground. Two hundred and forty hp made this rocket race through the streets like a shark under water.

When I climbed into the bucket seat and stroked over the curve of the wheel, I inhaled the scent of new leather and smirked. "Miss me, love?"

The answer came when I pushed the start button and softly tipped my foot on the gas pedal. The Audi gave a roar that would have made its big brothers go pale with envy. Man, I loved that sound. The garage's wide roll-up door opened at the push of the button on the small remote attached to my key ring. Sunlight streamed into the garage and blinded me. I grabbed my sunglasses that lay in the center console, shook them open with one hand, and put them on.

The music boomed from the speakers on a level meant for going deaf as I left the garage and our driveway to head down the road. In no time, the ride was over, because the soccer field was right next to our school, only two miles away from my house. On this Saturday morning, the parking lot was quite busy, which meant that more students had come to the tryouts than expected.

From the floorboard on the passenger side, I grabbed my backpack and threw it over one shoulder. Locking the car, I headed for the grounds.

There I spotted Torres, Frederickson, Sebastian Randall, and Alex. I had asked them to come help me sort through the girls today, kick around some ball with them, and judge their skills. Frederickson was our goalie, so he'd do what he always did. The rest of the crowd on the lawn was female. Since Tony wasn't here yet, I didn't even bother to look for Lisa, because she wouldn't come without him. I headed straight to the bench where about a million handbags and backpacks were parked, and one girl. While all the others did some stretching or chatting elsewhere, this one was actually reading a book.

She wasn't in any of my classes, nor had I ever gone out with her, but I knew she'd told me her name yesterday at Charlie's. Heck, what was it again?

I dumped my stuff next to her and said, "Hi."

She looked up from her book and took off her metal-rimmed glasses. "Hey."

"Good story?"

"Fantastic." Then she blushed an awful red and grimaced, probably because she'd just caught my subtle taunting. It was weird to go to soccer tryouts to read a book. "I only have half a chapter left, and I just couldn't stop."

She was sweet, this one. "Go finish your chapter. I still need a few minutes to get everything ready, anyway."

She seemed totally happy with my words, putting her glasses back on and her nose back in the book, which made me shake my head but chuckle as I fished for the list of names in my backpack. Running my forefinger from top to bottom, I looked for the name that I'd jotted down below Elisabeth MacKenzie, because I was pretty sure this girl had been sitting right next to her in the café. Yep, there it was. *Miller*. That was her.

Sitting down beside her, I traded my shoes for my cleats. An airy thud next to my ear said she'd finished her book. "How are you going to go about this?"

Making a knot with the loops of my tied laces, I tilted my head to look up at her. "What do you mean?"

"Well, there are way over fifty girls wanting on your team. How do you choose between us?"

I moved to my other shoe and started lacing it. "Dunno. Let you kick some goals and stuff. Watch you play."

"Tough job with so many girls," she replied and put her book in one of the million backpacks lying around. "Do you have a rating system?"

No, I didn't. Because I thought there would be fifteen to choose between, maybe twenty. I didn't reckon on half the school. I quirked my brows at her, chewing on my bottom lip.

"That means no, right?"

"No. Right."

She laughed at that. "Maybe you should give points for certain things and then just take the girls with the highest scores?"

That sounded like a brilliant idea. "You're a smart one." I stood and gave her one of those smirks I usually saved for *asking-a-girl-out* moments. It was okay, because those moments had become rare, anyway. The only sheet I had with me, though, was full of names, and there was no room left for taking any sort of notes. "You wouldn't by any chance have—"

"A notebook?" she finished for me, giving me the same mocking tone I had used on her before. By her grin, it was apparent she had one, indeed. She handed me the notebook together with a pen.

Yeah, that was perfect. I placed the book on a small table in front of the bleachers and moved a second bench closer so that I could sit down for writing. The girl came over and gave me a hand with the bench. "Thanks," I told her.

She nodded then walked out to the field. It was rare that any girl managed to get into my good-zone so fast, but she was a nice one, smart and helpful. "Hey, Susan!" I shouted after her.

As she stopped and turned around, there was this quirky look of surprise on her face. "Yes...Ryan?"

Ah, it was the fact that I knew her name that caught her off guard. I chuckled. I certainly wouldn't forget it again. "Would you care to help me with the notes? I just think I should be more on the field instead of sitting here writing things down."

Susan came back to me and looked me sternly in the eyes with her arms folded angrily over her flat chest. "You want me to be your *secretary*?"

"Ugh-ph..." I hadn't meant to offend her, and to be fair, I had no idea what to reply to that.

Luckily, her cute face scrunched with a smile then, and she swatted me on the shoulder. "Just kidding, Hunter. Of course I'll help you."

I laughed and rolled my eyes. Yeah. *Definitely* liked her.

We discussed that she'd rasterize the sheet and in the end just add up the scores at the bottom. Her notebook turned out to be a grab bag of surprises, because she ripped two pages from the very back that had square stickers on them and gave them to me. "You write a number on each of these and have the girls stick them on their asses or wherever. It'll be easier to work the scores out this way."

She gave me another pen and, like a real assistant, shooed me off to get started.

The girls lined up, and one by one they took a sticker with a number from me, while I shouted the matching names over to Susan. Chloe was one of the first, and her friend, Brinna, of course grabbed the number that followed. By the time I'd given out over thirty stickers, the queue had only halved. It was amazing just how many girls at our school wanted to play soccer.

"Forty-five, Higgins! Forty-six, Stevenson! Forty-seven..." I

ANNA KATMORE

looked up to see who was next and found myself face to face with the girl who dominated ninety-nine percent of my thoughts. "Matthews."

CHAPTER 4

IT WAS NICE to see that Lisa mirrored my smile with one of her own. She hadn't done that before, ever. Not that I had smiled at her a lot so far, or that we'd had any eye contact other than a passing look in the school hallways. Not wearing a cap seemed to have been a good idea, because her gaze so obviously wandered up to my chaotic hairstyle then snapped back to my face as though she was caught ogling. I didn't mind. If she liked what she saw, she could happily stare at me all day.

With a confident feeling in my gut, I decided that things were going to change today. *Radically.*

"Good luck, Matthews." I gave her the sticker, which she popped on the upper curve of her left boob, and rubbed it smooth.

Holy penalty kick, she shouldn't be doing this to me. My eyes fastened on that same spot while my mouth watered so badly I was afraid I wouldn't be able to say anything else without drooling all over her.

Fortunately, she didn't pay attention to my sudden lack of composure but turned around and headed back to Tony. Pulling myself together fast, I nodded a greeting at my friend then cleared my throat...several times. "Okay, everybody. For a little warm-up, I want you to run three laps around the field then come back here," I shouted over the murmurs.

After some protesting moans, the crowd got moving. Susan left her post to join in the warm-up, and I jogged over to run with her. "Thanks for your help," I told her. "That's really cool of you."

"Yeah, sure. No problem." She gasped for air as we ran then continued, "As long as that gives me a special status for the tryouts, we're fine."

That made me laugh. In fact, I was thinking about it already. Though I had no idea how she'd handle the ball, I thought it would be fun to have an upfront girl like her on the team. "Don't you worry about that, Miller. If you can hit a ball with your foot, we're good."

I left her side after the first lap and sat on the small table with Alex and Frederickson, watching how some of the girls already fought for air.

"Tony's girl is going to collapse before she makes the three rounds," Frederickson stated, and I automatically scanned the girls for Chloe. But she ran like a pro. Then, of course, to everyone else, Tony's girl would still be Lisa. I found her crawling more so than jogging next to Mitchell. She was totally red in the face and panting like a tank engine.

"That's not good," I mumbled.

"Why?" Alex wanted to know.

"Because last night Tony asked me to take her on the team." And of course, I would have done so even if I had to give her a piggyback ride just to finish the warm-up.

"Well then, I guess you have to be gentle on her." Alex laughed and pushed away from the table. Something told me that his joke was, in fact, on me.

After most of the girls had finished the three laps, I started a goal drill. Everybody had to score at least once. Three points if the first kick was a goal. None if they didn't manage to get the ball past Frederickson even on the third try. Of course, Frederickson wasn't giving his best today. It was more like fifteen percent of what he was capable of. But we didn't want to win a match today, we wanted to restock the team, so fifteen percent was good.

I got a little excited as numbers forty to forty-six took their turns. Next would be Lisa, and I couldn't wait to practice shooting with her. But when I turned around, she was sitting on the ground talking to Mitchell, who handed her a drink in a paper cup. I had always been cool with him being her companion, best friend, playmate, whatever. It had gotten on my nerves, but I had never said a word. However, since last night—since Tony had told me he was seriously involved with Chloe—I was more jealous than ever. At their tiniest touch, the urge to hit something hard rose within me. This was a serious problem, and I could only hope that Mitchell would come out with the truth fast. She would see him with different eyes then. With eyes that didn't bear this romantic, dreamy, *take-me-now* look any longer.

"Matthews! Your turn!" I yelled, suppressing my jealousy,

and kicked the ball toward her. She turned around and caught the ball to her chest. Good reflexes. There was definitely some potential in that, even if she'd used her hands.

I waited next to the goal while she placed the ball in the grass then kicked it with mild power toward Frederickson. He didn't have to move an inch to stop the ball. In fact, it died on the way to the goal, looking like it needed resuscitation. So, shooting wasn't Lisa's strength, either.

"Come on, Matthews!" I shouted as I picked up the ball and jogged over to her. She looked like she was going to surrender. Sweat coated every inch of her skin and breathing still troubled her after running the three laps. But I couldn't let her fail in this qualifying exercise, so I tried to tickle out her ambition with a smirk. "I've seen you kick Mitchell's butt harder than that."

Since she didn't back off, I guessed she was up to another try, so I dropped the ball in front of her. Then I placed my hands on her shoulders and moved her several steps back. "Now take a short run and put a little more power in your thrust."

This was the first time that I'd ever touched Lisa Matthews. And I thanked God for the invention of tank tops. Her skin was smooth and heated, emitting the warm scent of some flower mix. I didn't know what she rubbed on her body after a shower, but the smell of it drove me crazy and close to not giving a fuck about who might see it if I went and kissed the girl in another moment.

Unfortunately, she didn't look very happy about my touch.

She grabbed the collar of Tony's jersey and whined, "Ah no, don't let him make me do that. We both know I'll just trip over the damn thing."

She looked so hilariously panicky that I couldn't stop myself from laughing while Tony pried her fingers loose from his collar. "No, you won't," he told her in a confident way. Then he shot me a quick glance that looked like he was asking my permission for…something. I nodded, because I trusted him fully. Anyway, we both wanted the same thing today, which was getting Lisa on the team. "Tell you what, if you hit Frederickson straight in the chest, I'll buy you a chocolate decadence ice cream sundae," he tempted her. "Deal?"

It wouldn't be a goal if the ball didn't make it *past* Frederickson, but as long as the outcome at the end of the day was the same, I didn't care.

Lisa considered the new task for a second then grinned. "Deal." She ran two steps then kicked the ball with honorable strength. It dropped like a baby in Frederickson's arms. At least she'd mastered the new task.

"Well done!" I told her, wishing I would be the one to buy her ice cream later.

I returned to the table and to Susan. "Forty-seven gets three points for the goal shooting," I told her. She'd seen what happened, and of course it earned me a quizzical look from the book lover, but I was the captain of this team, and what I said was law. It only took my arching one brow to make her understand that, and she scribbled a perfect "3" next to Lisa's name. When she grinned up at me in a nice, schoolgirl manner, I did the same. I liked how we communicated without words and understood each other so well.

I finished the goal exercise with the remaining players then joined my buddies Alex and Sasha, who were practicing dribbling across the lawn and passing with some of the girls. Tony did the same with Lisa, and though she wasn't a pro, she managed a few very promising passes to Mitchell. I watched them for a while, deciding whether to give her the deserved two points in this drill or the full five. And she was *really* lame at the next exercise, which tested their balance and skills at juggling the ball with one leg, doing kicks without dropping it. I grimaced and dragged my hands down over my face. There was no need to even start counting how many she could do.

I scratched my head. If I gave her a fair rating, she'd never make it on the team. There were at least thirty other girls better than her. On the plus side, she wasn't the worst, so having her on the team wouldn't turn out to be a total loss.

On the way over to Susan, a sneak attack made me drop to all fours. One of the girls had hit me at the back of my left knee with a really hard kick that Alex had failed to stop. Me going down like a shot buffalo caused a round of laughter and some taunting from Alex. It took exactly two seconds until he was on the ground underneath me, and we wrestled around like young dogs.

"Hey, Sash," Frederickson yelled above us. "Help me get the kids apart. They're always so *hyped up* when they get coffee in the morning."

Alex and I each grabbed one of Frederickson's legs, which was his downfall.

"Oh, come on, guys." I heard Chloe's annoyed voice. "Can you wait until later with the wrestling? Some of us would like to know if we're on the team."

I wrestled myself free from Alex and Frederickson and gave Chloe a wry look. "You got the maximum score in every event, Summers. I guess it's okay to say that you probably made it."

She disappeared on a happy skip, and I could finally tell Susan the last few scores to enter onto her list. I walked up behind her, braced my palms on the wooden top on either side of her, and leaned over her shoulder. Susan gave a short gasp, probably at the unexpected nearness. If I'd judged her right, she'd never had a boy touch her, let alone kiss her. Dating might not be important in her books. That was a shame. She was cool and she smelled like vanilla milk. She had a pretty face, even with her glasses. The only thing missing on this one was boobs, but she was only sixteen. They might come soon.

I pointed to the bottom of the list. "Fifty-three and four get three points each for dribbling and passing, and they did seven and ten at the juggling. There's no need to write anything down for numbers fifty-six, seven, and eight. They won't make it."

"Okay, so we have all of them. Well...all but one." She tilted her head a little and studied me from the corner of her eye. "You didn't give me the scores for Lisa Matthews."

"Didn't I?" It was a suggestive drawl, and it made Susan chuckle.

"Let me guess, five points for dribbling and passing, and at juggling she probably did an imaginary...*twelve*?"

"Fifteen."

She pointed the tip of her pen at me. "Right." Then she wrote the numbers on the list without further discussion, but she wore a knowing smile all the time.

I leaned lower to speak into her ear. "You know, as my personal assistant, you're bound to secrecy."

"Absolutely," she confirmed with the same sneer I wore, and for some reason I knew I could trust her with that. When she was done writing, I took her hand and pulled her off the bench. "Okay, it's your turn now, book lover. Let's see what you can do with a ball." As my unofficial secretary, she hadn't had much time to take part in the tryouts, so I ran her personally through the drills. She probably wasn't going to be a professional soccer player, not now or ever. But she was better than Lisa at most things, and even though her scores sucked, I put Susan's name on the new members list.

Her shadow moved over the paper when she leaned forward to take a look at what I wrote. Then she straightened with that quirky grin again. "You know, some people say you're an ass, Hunter. I can't see why that is."

"That's because they don't know me." I winked at her then headed to the middle of the field and welcomed the new members. When Lisa realized she'd made it, her sweet mouth hung open like she was trying to catch fish with it. Apparently, it took Mitchell a minute to assure her that she hadn't heard wrong. Happy like a kitten, she hurried to the bench and fished around for her backpack.

I followed her. Step one of courting my dream girl was a success. She was on my team now. Step two: invite her to my party.

I intended to say *hi* when I stood right behind her, but at the same moment, she whirled around so fast that she bumped straight into my chest, throwing me a step back. Cupping her elbows, I prevented her from tripping. And once again, I couldn't resist taking a deep breath of the beautiful scent that clung to her hair and body. "Congrats, Matthews," I said. "You handled the tryouts quite well."

She only gave me a mean growl. "Yeah, whatever." I was so stunned that I didn't even hold her back when she strode past me, with a pissed glare on her face. But then she stopped and spun on her heel, folding her arms defiantly over her chest. "What does Tony owe you for putting me on the team?"

Whoa. That, I sure didn't expect. Hell, what to do now? Lie to her? Give her the truth? Grab her by her neck and just haul her into me for a distracting kiss? I would so go for the last option, but it didn't seem like something that would work to my advantage. So I did what I felt like and laughed, deciding for the almost-truth. "You don't want to know."

Obviously, she did, and by the look on her face, she was

ready to beat it right out of me if necessary. I decided I might tell her why I put her on the team...one day. For now, it was better to pull my head out of the noose. I turned around and started walking away, but then I remembered the one thing that had brought me over to her in the first place. I cast her a look over my shoulder that suggested she'd better not say no. "See you at my house, Matthews."

She nailed me with her baffled gaze, and that was everything I needed. She'd be there tonight. And in my house it would be my rules. She didn't know it yet, but she wouldn't stand a chance. In the end, she'd be mine.

Smiling to myself like a lovesick fool, I grabbed my backpack and headed for my car.

I had only reversed out of the spot and turned onto the road, when I spotted Susan Miller walking on the pavement. She was the only new member on our team who hadn't been at my house yet, and I had totally forgotten to give her an invitation for tonight's party. Slowing down to match her pace, I rolled the passenger window down and leaned forward a little, so I could see her face. "Hey, book lover!"

She didn't stop but turned her head in my direction. "Hi, there."

"Need a ride?"

Taken aback, she raised one brow, something I knew I did a lot and it was weird to see it on someone else's face. "Um...no thanks. It's not that far."

"Would you get in, anyway? I need to talk to you."

As she stopped, I did, too. She looked up the road then back at me. "I guess that's okay." With her backpack on her lap, Susan sat down in the passenger seat and buckled herself in. "What's up?"

"I forgot to tell you something," I began as I pulled away from the curb and cruised up the street. "Where are we going?"

"Half a mile this way, then turn onto Rasmussen Avenue. So what did you want to talk about? If it's about the cheating with Lisa's scores, you don't have to worry. She's my friend, I won't tell anybody."

"Okay, that's good to know then." This was, in fact, the other thing I really felt the need to discuss with Susan. "Mitchell asked me to bring her on, so it's a personal favor. Matthews doesn't have to know that. I don't want her to feel bad because of it."

She nodded like she totally understood, but then she sucked her bottom lip between her teeth and started chewing on it. I cut her a glance through speculative slits. "What?"

"Nothing."

I chuckled, because it sure wasn't nothing. "Come on, you can say it."

"Yeah, maybe I can. I mean, I'm sitting in this hot car with you, something half the school will envy me for if I tell them, right? And I have no idea why I'm here, but it's cool so...I'll be honest. I was wondering if it really was *only* a favor for Tony."

"What, taking Matthews onto the team?"

"Yep."

I felt a grin tugging on the corners of my mouth as I quickly glanced at her from the corner of my eye. "What makes you think otherwise?" I looked back at the street, but I knew she was staring at me openly now, because she'd shifted in the seat to face me.

"The way you checked out Lisa's butt while she was running, for instance." She made it sound like a suggestion, but then she added quickly. "Unless you were checking out *Tony's* butt, which I seriously hope you weren't. And then I saw you sniffing your hands in a very weird, very romantic way after you touched her, which made me think you like how she smells."

The more she said, the wider my smile grew. "Were you spying on me, book lover?"

"Is it bad to say I watched you?" she whined. "I was just curious to see what you'd do today after you so secretly flirted with her yesterday."

I gulped as I turned onto Rasmussen Avenue. "It certainly wasn't that much of a secret if you noticed it." And then Frederickson and Alex had, too.

Now she gave a sigh. Something dreamy and longing. "I guess I'm just spoiled in that way. I read so many romance books that I can smell it from ten miles away when a guy is falling for a girl."

"*Falling* for her?" My voice held a hint of defensive accusation, so much so that I probably sounded as if I'd been caught red-handed. Enough that she knew she was dead on.

"Don't panic. Like I said, I'm not telling anybody. And Lisa certainly isn't aware of it just yet. Could you stop here? The yellow house is mine."

Bringing the car to a halt in front of her yard, I watched her unfasten the seat belt and said, "I guess I'll be seeing you in the evening." As she lifted her head and gave me a questioning look, I added, "At the party? You're coming, right?"

The next second, I realized she was just winding me up again, because her expression turned sickly romantic and she hugged her backpack dreamily to her chest. "Oh Hunter, I thought you would never ask."

Rolling my eyes, I had to laugh about the way she made me look. Crazy chick.

She climbed out and slammed the door shut then walked up the front steps. "Hey, book lover!" I shouted after her and waited until she turned around. "It's nice to have you on the team."

Susan's eyes wrinkled behind her glasses as she smiled. Then she walked inside, and I stepped on the gas, heading home.

All afternoon I was busy getting the house ready for the party of the year. I didn't need to wait for responses to my text. Everyone who had time would come and have a little fun tonight.

I got all the expensive carpets out of the way so that only the naked stone tiles were left. From the credenzas and shelves, I removed everything that could be broken, and also Mom's

ANNA KATMORE

beloved Chinese Ming vase that stood close to the French doors leading into our garden. When Dad came in after work, he helped me drape some blankets over the leather couch and replace the glass coffee table with an old chest that would do the job just as well, before he and Mom gave me the usual sermon on the party rules and then left for Mary Fisher's house. In the end, our entrance hall and front room looked like the Hunters had moved out, but only until the first bunch of guests arrived. Everyone had free access to drinks and food, and while they made themselves at home and put some music on, I headed upstairs to finally change for the night.

I slipped into my favorite faded blue jeans with the ripped hems and found my tennis shoes under my bed. After styling my hair in a David Beckham style Mohawk, I picked a white shirt from the closet, but as soon as I had it on, I unbuttoned it again and threw it on my bed. White clashed with my dark hair too much to look cool. A black dress shirt would do. I let it casually hang out and rolled the sleeves up to my elbows as I stepped in front of the mirror again. Yep, much better.

The music switched from Nickleback to Bob Marley's "Stop That Train" as I closed the door to my room and headed downstairs. A funny memory came up with that song. I was about ten years old when Justin had stolen a cigar from his granddad and we tried to smoke it in the gazebo in our garden. The outcome wasn't all that pretty. In fact, after the second drag, we both went green in the face and puked into my mom's rose bushes. Yeah, we were so cool...

I wondered if Justin was the one fumbling with the hi-fi, because the song was suddenly cut off after the first few beats, and Sean Paul came on next. "She Doesn't Mind." I liked that one.

When I came down, Claudia Wesley ran into me. Narrowly escaping getting splattered by the drink in her hand, I steadied her by her elbows, and her face lit up. "Hunter, you're late to your own party? That is so like you."

"You know me. I can't be on time to save my life." I had gone out with Claudia in tenth grade, and if it had ever worked with a girl and me, then it was probably her. The only downside—she wasn't Lisa. But she made a fantastic wine cooler, and the glass in her hand was most likely filled with the stuff. I took it out of her hand and tasted the berry mix, then arched a brow at her. "That grog could kill an elephant."

She shrugged it off with a grin. "Yeah, it's a little strong. But the strawberries make it perfect."

It tasted delicious, but I didn't intend to get drunk tonight, so I gave the glass back to her. The house was already bursting. I had to fight my way through all the kids to get into the kitchen and grab a beer from the fridge. The lights had been dimmed and the music was at maximum volume, just what a good party needed. I popped the cap of the Corona and headed back to the hall, taking a swig.

In the arch between the hall and the kitchen, Tony bumped into me, dragged by a very excited Chloe. "Hey guys, what are *you* up to?" I asked, amused about how they held hands like preschoolers, and seriously enjoying the fact that Tony seemed totally into that girl.

"I want to show him the gazebo," Chloe squeaked. "You don't mind, Hunter, do you?"

I shook my head no, but caught Mitchell's arm before Chloe could pull him away from me. Leaning in closer, I gave him a concerned look. "Did you come with Matthews?"

"Yes."

My eyes widened as I glanced from him to Chloe and back. "And she knows you're going to make out with someone else in my garden?"

Tony sucked in an uneasy breath through his teeth. "No."

Yeah, that was to be foreseen. "Where is she?"

"Somewhere back there." He nodded over his shoulder toward the front door. "A friend held her up. Look, I won't be out with Chloe long. Just a minute. Don't tell Lisa when you see her, okay?"

Chloe impatiently blew a strand of her blonde hair out of her eyes, but I made a point of not letting go of Mitchell's arm just yet. "You will have to tell her at some point."

"I know." He grimaced. "I will."

"All right. Get along with you," I growled. "I have you covered for tonight. But make sure to come clean with her soon. I hate lying."

"Thanks, man." We bumped fists before the two of them slipped out into the garden through the back door.

I wondered how he'd gotten Chloe to agree to hiding their

relationship for now. She wasn't usually one to keep a low profile and it must've been annoying the hell out of her. But then, our garden was a perfectly romantic place for some kissing under the moonlight, and she would probably get her money's worth with Mitchell tonight.

A little frustrated at how Tony was messing with Lisa's feelings, I slumped against the wall inside the arch, dragged a hand over my face, and took a long sip from my beer. Gaze skating over the crowd, I wondered where she was. There were close to three hundred people in this house. Looking for her might turn out to be difficult. But then, there was no need to. The little hairs at the back of my neck bristled when she emerged from the mass, glancing around like a shy little doe.

Her super short, black pants took a millisecond to make my eyes go wide and my mouth water. A moment after her gaze met mine, I turned toward her fully, leaning only one shoulder against the wall. She fumbled with the hem of her gray tank top as she glanced to one side and back at me. From years of charming girls, I knew what I was doing. Since she had my direct attention now, she had no other choice than to come over and say hello. I took another swig as I watched my plan work.

Near enough to grant me a close-up of the pendant on her necklace dipping into the valley between her breasts, she stopped and lifted a hand in greeting instead of speaking.

I cocked my head and gave her the lightest smile I could manage. "Hi."

"You have a nice place. So full of—"

ANNA KATMORE

Testosterone?

"—people."

"Yeah. Thanks." Hm, was that the right thing to say? I pushed away from the wall and leaned in a little closer, because I hated to shout over the music. Okay, the music wasn't so loud back here, so it might not have been *only* that. I also really liked to breathe in the sweet scent of her shampoo. Her hair tickled my cheek when I lowered my head even more to speak into her ear. "It was about time Mitchell brought you here. He kept you away from this place long enough."

Her nose brushed the underside of my jaw, giving me a really good feeling in my stomach. "Do you know where he is?"

Sorry, baby, but I can't tell you that. Looking down, I only saw her perfect, apple-shaped boobs and a waist that begged to be hugged against mine. The bottle of beer in my hand gave me a chance to hold onto something as I fought against the urge to grab what I had already determined was mine. "Nope," I answered her question then washed away the bitter aftertaste of the lie with a swig of Corona.

Lisa had her own bottle of beer and drank when I did, but she looked like it was the nastiest stuff one could've given her. I wondered if she'd gotten it from Tony, but I was pretty sure he made a point of keeping this girl sober.

Our fridge was stocked with things that tasted better than Corona, and I didn't like the thought of her getting tipsy at my party, anyway. At least no one had given her a glass of the strawberry wine cooler. That stuff would have knocked her out of her shoes.

With her wrist in my hand, I pulled her away from the hall and into the kitchen to trade her beer for a soda. Touching her actually felt so good that I couldn't bring myself to let her go immediately, so I put my bottle on the counter and worked one-handed to pop open a can of Sprite for her. Replacing the bottle with the can, I made an effort to gently close her fingers around it.

"You shouldn't drink beer," I told her and hoped I didn't sound like her dad or something. "Especially not in this place."

Thankfully, she wasn't pissed at my parenting her. In fact, she looked happy about the new drink and sipped from it while I still held her discarded bottle. I leaned my butt against the counter and crossed my legs at the ankles. "You did really well today," I offered as an icebreaker for an easier chat.

She swallowed the hook, but she knew I was being polite—and not very honest. "I was lousy. And you know it. I still don't get why you chose me to play on your team."

Yeah, *why?* I gave a nonchalant shrug and drank from her bottle. Jeez, I had my mouth on the same spot her lips had just touched. It might be childish, but I enjoyed that moment like nothing else before. Then I drawled, "I don't know. Maybe I just want you there." My teasing added a spark to her shiny green eyes. I liked how I could give her a coating of goose bumps with just this tiny bit of truth. "Do a little endurance training every day, and you'll be a capable player."

"I guess I'm lacking the motivation to do that. I'm like a

lame duck at running."

Is that so? Hm, what could we do about that? "What you need is a personal trainer."

The pretty girl in front of me laughed and took a short step back, studying me with disbelieving eyes. "You want the job?"

That was why I suggested it. But I played my cool role to perfection. "Sure, why not? If you promise to show some enthusiasm, I promise to be there."

She tilted her head and narrowed her eyes a little. I couldn't blame her for not trusting me just yet. We were only getting acquainted with each other. Lisa wasn't someone you rushed into your bed. She was a gem that you enjoyed marveling at. If you were lucky, you got the chance to touch her delicate surface. A treasure that I'd go to any length to make my own.

Eventually, she said, "Okay, deal."

Deal? That was a fucking *yes* to a date. I felt like an idiot from one of Susan Miller's romance books when my heart actually did some sort of backflip in my chest. I struggled to stay cool but managed to keep my pleasure under control and just nodded. "We'll start Monday morning."

She didn't look so happy anymore. Hopefully, she didn't regret her decision already. Regardless, I wouldn't let her go back on her word, and I made that clear by trapping her gaze with a hot, determined look. If she got her foot into this game with me, she wouldn't get out of it single. I wanted her to be aware of whom she was dealing with, because I'd never felt as true to the name Bay Shark as I did in this moment.

"Hey, Ryan! We're starting a game of pool. Are you in?"

Fuck you, Justin! I wanted to strangle my friend for ruining this moment for me. I glared over Lisa's shoulder at him, and he sure knew right then that he'd come at the entirely wrong moment.

"Sorry, man," he mouthed and grimaced.

Exhaling a sigh, I pushed away from the counter. The spell was over. I might as well go play pool with my friends now. But I was going to train with Lisa on Monday. I had been waiting years for that chance, so what was one more day? "There in a sec," I told Justin.

When he was gone and I looked at Lisa's beautiful face again, I wondered what that sweet mouth of hers would taste like. I stroked her cheek with the neck of my bottle. And there it was—the first dreamy look in her eyes that was *only* for me.

"Enjoy the night," I said in quite a soft way. "And whatever you do, stay away from the strawberries."

It was time to go, or I would do something stupid way too early in my plan for seducing Lisa. So I headed for the door, leaving her a little stunned. But when I stepped past her, I couldn't resist stroking the back of her hand with my own.

ANNA KATMORE

CHAPTER 5

A FEW GUYS stood around the pool table. Justin was playing a game against Alex when I came into the room adjoining the main hall. Justin looked up and his face crumpled worse than a raisin. "Ah man, sorry, that wasn't my intention," he apologized again, straightening and leaning on his cue.

"Forget it." I grinned. "It's all set for Monday."

That made him lift his brows in an impressed way and nod.

"What's set for Monday?" Alex demanded after he shot the yellow ball into a hole. "And what wasn't your intention, Juz?"

"Nothing," Justin and I shot back at him.

"Is there money in the pot?" I tried to change the topic as I sat down on the couch between Frederickson and a guy whose real name I didn't know but who we all called Sylvester.

Alex tapped the stack of dollar bills on the table with the tip of his cue. "Twenty-five from each."

"I'll play the winner." I didn't have to play for money to stock up my bank account, but it was way more fun playing with the guys if *they* had the right incentive. For one, they didn't play pool like sissies then.

It wasn't easy to tell who was the better player, but this

time Justin came out the winner, because Alex sank the eight ball early.

"Fifty's in the pot," Justin said to me with a wide sneer. "I want to see your money if you want to play."

I pulled two twenties and a ten from my wallet and placed them on Justin's prize money. "I'm in."

Alex passed me the cue, and I chalked it while someone else racked the balls for us. Because I'd only just come in, I got to shoot first. Number twelve ended in the left corner pocket, which left Justin with solids and me with stripes. It was a fast game. In only four turns I had dumped most of my balls. Only the orange and white ball—number thirteen—was left, and I holed it into a corner pocket with a spectacular shot over three cushions. Now just the eight ball, and victory would be mine.

My confident smirk at Justin made the guy a little nervous. "Come on, Ryan, give a friend a chance. You can't hole the ball just yet," he whined.

That didn't irritate me. "What's your problem, Justin? Afraid your mama's going to find out you're playing for money?" I leaned forward, focusing on the black ball, measuring my final shot.

"My mama doesn't give a damn. But I *really, really* need this *Spiderman* comic. It's an original."

Ah, right. With Justin, if it wasn't about BMX or girls, it was always comics. He hoarded them like squirrels hoarded nuts, and I couldn't believe how much he was willing to spend on those books when his pocket money for a year was what I got in a month.

He had me feeling bad for him...almost. Heck, this was a guy thing, and I couldn't lose just to make a friend happy. When you're eighteen, it's all about rep.

I positioned the cue in a perfect line with the white ball, the eight, and the left corner pocket. I was so close to winning this game. Only, I made the mistake of looking up for a second and froze.

For an immeasurable moment, I forgot to breathe. How dare she come in here and ruin this game for me? Ah *God*, how dare she look so good? It only took a second for the others to realize something had gone wrong, and they all turned to find my personal downfall standing in the doorway.

Lisa grimaced and played uncomfortably with the hem of her top. "Is something wrong?"

Everything was wrong. It always was with me when this girl was anywhere near. The day I had first seen Lisa Matthews, I'd tripped over the soccer ball and landed face first in the dirt. She always made me forget about anything else around me. And now, she'd cost me a fair sum if she didn't turn around and walk out so I could get my head back in the game.

No such luck. Justin made sure of that. He rushed to her side, the grin of victory sitting fat on his face. "You just saved my life, hun."

Lisa seemed a little surprised when Justin laid his arm around her shoulders and pulled her farther into the room where the warm light from above played up the various shades of brown in her hair. I wanted to kick my best friend's ass at this moment because, for one, he knew I'd screw up with Lisa in the room and he was using that to his advantage. And secondly, because he dared to lay his fucking arm around my girl. He was going to pay for *both* later.

"Ah...yes," Lisa said and looked from Justin to me. "And how so?"

She had *no* idea. That was one of the things I liked about her most—that she was always so sweetly unaware of everything. Especially of the crap that was just about to fall on my head.

"He can't play when someone is watching him," Justin stated the obvious. "Totally screws up then."

Her brows knitted together. "But you *all* are watching him."

The way she spoke to everybody else but looked only at me made me grin.

"Yeah, but we're not girls." That was Alex from the back of the room, and he certainly enjoyed selling me out. Bastards. Were they all against me tonight?

It was probably time to say something in my defense, to save my honor, but all I did was fix Lisa with a salacious stare as I straightened and chalked the tip of my cue.

"Sorry," she croaked. "I'll leave you guys alone then."

Justin didn't let her slip away. "Uh-uh, no way, hun! You're my insurance of getting that comic book. You stay."

His arm around her got mightily on my nerves, even

though he made Lisa smile. And heck, she had the prettiest smile in all of Grover Beach. One that conjured sweet dimples on her cheeks and made her pretty green eyes crinkle. One that made me lick my bottom lip, wanting nothing more than to kiss her.

And because she was still only gazing at me and no one else as she smiled, I couldn't help that one corner of my mouth tilted up. I was in serious trouble. Lisa distracted me something awful. She made me lose my mind and she was about to make me lose this game, too. More importantly, she'd made me lose face in front of my closest friends—and yet she still lived. *Damn, I must be in love with this girl.*

Taking a deep breath, I shook my head and leaned over the table once more. Everybody was tense and silent. They would've just loved to see me butcher this shot. I cleared my throat, playing for more time, hoping for a miracle that would swipe Lisa out of the room this second. But she remained, and I couldn't stop looking at her. Hard as I tried to concentrate on the balls in front of me, my gaze drifted up to her face time and time again.

Ah, to hell with it! This game was lost.

I dropped my forehead to the edge of the table and laughed. "Take your money, Andrews. I give up."

The boys broke out in a rowdy cheer. *Yeah, right, rub it in guys!*

Bracing my palms on the pool table, I hung my head for a moment, accepting their gloating. But when I looked up, Lisa was still there capturing me with her gaze, and I knew it was totally worth it.

"I'm so sorry," she mouthed.

And she'd better be. Lisa probably had no idea how badly she'd damaged my rep and that the boys would never let me live this down. But I wasn't angry. How could I be? She was the sweetest distraction that had ever walked through my door.

I didn't let her out of my sight but smirked and mouthed back, "*You* are banned from this room."

She didn't move an inch when I slowly walked around the table toward her. In fact, she even pressed a little harder against the wall, her eyes growing wider, her breathing coming just a bit faster. It looked like she couldn't make up her mind whether she should shy away from me or be fascinated.

I stood only half a foot away from her, with the cue tight in one hand. The other I placed against the wall next to her head so she couldn't escape me. "You just cost me fifty bucks."

"Yeah, I know. But he *really, really* needs this comic book." She batted her long lashes at me. To my shame, I had to admit that this simple move bulldozed right through my coolness.

I laughed. "Siding with the enemy. I should have known." Then I seized the opportunity to touch her one more time tonight and placed my hand in the small of her back. "For tonight, this room is off limits for you." Gently, I pushed her through the door back into the main hall and enjoyed every second my hand lay on her warm body.

"Oh why? It's so much fun to watch you...screw up."

She mockingly glanced up at me, and I should have bitten her bottom lip for that impish pout.

But I resisted that urge and also the one to brush my thumb over her lip. Instead, I leaned in a little closer. "Off you go."

She obeyed, and I didn't know if that made me happy or sad. But as soon as she was gone, I closed the sliding wood door and slumped with my back against it, facing a hoard of sneering guys.

"Can anybody tell me why I never have my phone ready to record when things like that happen?" Chris Donovan popped open a new bottle of beer and saluted into the room. "Hunter screwing up a game because of Lisa Matthews. This is priceless."

"Mitchell is so going to kill you for stealing his girl," Alex said while rearranging the balls on the green felt.

"Mitchell doesn't have to know," I sneered back. "Anyway, I'm not stealing her. That was just some harmless flirting. Nothing to blow a fuse about."

"What *she* did was harmless. What *you* did, man, was begging on your knees to get laid."

A laugh escaped me at the honesty and probable truth in that. "Fuck you, Winter. Are we playing pool now or what?"

"You just epically failed. I'm not playing *you*, Hunter." He cast me a mocking glare then turned around. "Frederickson, get your ass off the couch. We're playing."

I shoved his shoulder for that last remark, and Alex laughed as he grabbed the edge of the pool table for balance.

Donovan hoisted himself onto the mini-bar, feet dangling, and leaned forward to rest his elbows on his thighs. The fat silver chain around his neck slipped out from under the collar of his T-shirt and swayed back and forth. "I never knew you felt anything for the chick."

Jeez, I'd have preferred if we didn't discuss my feelings and just continued with a nice evening of playing pool. "I'm not saying I do."

"Right, that's what you have us for," Alex said, still struggling to stop laughing. "And, dude, you got it bad."

As if I didn't know that. When I cut a glance over to Justin, the only one in the room who had known from the start how I felt, he shrugged, clearly telling me that I had no choice but to face it with the guys.

Frederickson got to his feet, grabbed my cue, and placed a hand on my shoulder. "Sincere condolences, Hunter. That girl won't let you get within a yard of her."

Rubbing the back of my neck, I couldn't bite down a smirk. "I believe I was way closer than that just a couple of minutes ago."

"Oooh," a collective taunting echoed through the room. I hated it when the guys behaved like some silly chicks at a bachelorette party. But at eighteen, almost everything was worth making a fool of oneself. I'd totally be with them if the joke wasn't on me tonight.

ANNA KATMORE

I dropped to the couch and leaned my head on the back, dragging my hands over my face, mostly to cover my stupid grin. "Shut up, you fuckers."

Alex made tsking noises before his first shot, knocking the balls in all directions. "Language, dude." When none of the balls dropped into a pocket, he dumped his ass next to me and waited for Frederickson to take his shot. His long legs stretched out and crossed at the ankles, he cast me a sideways glance. "Seriously, you think you stand a chance with the chick? To me it looks like she's happy to be Mitchell's groupie forever."

At this point, I wasn't sure if determination and charm alone were enough to change Lisa's mind, but I was ready to die trying. By what she'd showed me tonight, she wasn't totally resistant to everything I said or did. Maybe the problem was just that she'd never considered a different future for herself than one with Anthony Mitchell's ring on her finger. But there were so many possibilities for her, if only she would open up. And I was definitely one of them.

"That's because she doesn't know what she's going to miss while running after him," I said to Alex.

"You're going to show her?"

"Yeah. Hunter's just the man for that," Chris pointed out with an impish waggling of his brows. "I bet he has her in his bed before the week's over."

"Twenty that she doesn't even let him kiss her in that time," Frederickson countered.

"Guys!" I shouted to get their attention then nailed them

all with a severe stare. "Don't you even *think* of making a wager on this. Matthews isn't a girl you fool around with to win a bet. First, because she's the friend of a friend. And second—" I paused then slowly lifted one corner of my mouth. "Because I would hate to see you lose your money, Frederickson."

That made the guys hoot and whistle, and they all wished me luck. I definitely needed it if I wanted to land Lisa.

A few minutes passed before everyone was cool again, and we could play pool for a little while without distraction. When we'd depleted the mini-bar down to just tonic water, I left the guys to grab some drinks. "Going to get beer. Anybody else want one?"

Alex said yes, and Justin ordered soda.

As I walked into the kitchen, my hands immediately fisted by my sides, and I had trouble unclenching my teeth. Lisa sat on the counter, and Mitchell stood between her dangling feet. At first look I thought they were kissing, and my heart hurt so bad that I wondered if someone should call an ambulance because I was suffering a cardiac arrest. Until I realized Chloe was with them and Lisa was apparently having some trouble sitting upright. I'd sent her off with Sprite. How the hell had she ended up drunk?

Chloe pulled on Mitchell's arm, but he didn't seem to be ready to go. "Anthony, you promised to dance with me," she nagged him.

And then, in spite of my rage over Tony standing so close to Lisa, I had to suppress a chuckle as Lisa iterated in the voice

ANNA KATMORE

of a preschooler, "*Anthony, you promised to dance with me.*"

That sure pissed Chloe off. "What's wrong with *her?*"

"She just had a little too much of the wine cooler," said Tony. "I'll be with you in a minute."

I was about to tell him he should go with her now and let me handle Lisa. In her condition, it wasn't a good idea to let her deal with Chloe and the crap she didn't know about them yet.

But at the same moment, Lisa's head dipped to his shoulder. "I'm so tired. Can we go home?" she whined.

Chloe took a step back and folded her arms over her chest, which threatened to jump out of her plastered-on black dress. "Aw, come on, Anthony. You're not going to leave already. It's only eleven. Take her upstairs to one of Hunter's guest rooms. She can sleep there."

Oh no.

"And not bother you any longer?" A moan came from Lisa who looked like she was already falling asleep on Tony's shoulder.

Not up to getting involved in the drama of the night, I walked up beside Mitchell and said, "You don't want to do that. In her state, she's not safe in any of the guest rooms. You know how the parties go on the later it gets." So what option did we have left? "Take her to my room."

"*What?*" Lisa and Tony shouted, Lisa suddenly sitting up straight with her eyes wide open. So much for getting her in my bed before the week was over.

"Don't be ridiculous, guys." I rolled my eyes as if the

thought of doing anything with Lisa was totally absurd. If they knew the truth, Tony wouldn't trust me one bit. "She'll be awake and gone before I even get upstairs." Unfortunately, that was also the truth.

Since Lisa was as drunk as a rum truffle, it was up to Mitchell to decide for her. He was, after all, her best friend and therefore responsible...somehow. But he hesitated.

"Hell, do it already, Anthony, and come back fast," Chloe demanded.

When Tony pressed his lips into a straight line, I thought he would never agree. But then he said, "Come on, Liz," and pulled her off the counter. With his arm around her waist, he steadied her and walked her to the door.

After only three steps, she slipped away from him and knocked against the fridge, bounced back, and stumbled. "Pardon me," she said as if the fridge had just grown a soul.

She was going to run into the counter next, so I wrapped my arms around her, pulling her tight against me. "Didn't I tell you to stay away from the strawberries?" I growled into her ear, immediately getting high on her beautiful scent.

"Strawberries? There was one in my last soda." The silly girl grinned like a loon. "It was yummy."

"Yummy, all right." I chuckled. Then I scooped her up. Lord, had I known that this was Heaven, I'd have tried to be a nicer guy in the past. Her body was light and soft, and her warmth seeped through my shirt, causing my skin to prickle. My hands lay on places that I wouldn't have dared to dream of

ANNA KATMORE

touching just a couple of days ago.

"I'll carry her to my room, Mitchell. You can grab her when you go. Or come back for her in the morning." Or...don't come back at all and just leave her with me.

"You sure?" Yep, he didn't trust me at all.

"Yes. Go dance with Chloe or she'll pester me next."

He looked at Summers, and she flashed a radiant grin at him. All right! The battle was won. Mitchell handed Lisa into my care. If she'd been *my* best friend, I wouldn't have done that.

Savoring every second of cuddling Lisa to my chest, I carried her upstairs. She wrapped her arms around my neck, and suddenly her head rested on my shoulder. I briefly closed my eyes and my jaw tightened as I struggled to stay cool.

"You don't like dancing with Chloe?" she murmured.

I touched my cheek to her brow. "Would you?"

"I don't like her, period."

That was obvious. "And I know exactly why that is."

"Really?"

I just wanted to tell her that everybody knew how she was in love with my buddy, but she distracted me when her nose brushed against my neck and she inhaled deeply. "You smell good," she said in her lovely, drunken ramble, and I knew that without the strawberries I would have never heard this from her lips.

It made me happy and I laughed, and though I would have loved to get her into a conversation where she could tell me all the other things she might like about me, I knew it was wrong, because she would hate me for it tomorrow. If she even remembered it then. "Time to go to bed, Matthews."

Opening the door to my room with Lisa in my arms wasn't an easy thing, but I managed it with my elbow and carried her over to my wide bed underneath the window. Before I laid her down, I hugged her a little tighter with the intention that whatever else happened, I'd always remember this wonderful moment where I held the girl I'd loved for years for the very first time.

When she snuggled up to my pillow and sniffed like she couldn't get enough of the scent on it, I smiled to myself. Then I pulled her shoes off, covered her bare legs with the quilt, and squatted down beside her, staring at her sweet, pale face. "You comfortable?"

Her eyes were closed as she made a whiny face. "I'm not sure. But can you check if my head has sprouted helicopter blades?"

I stroked her soft, straight hair, brushing the long bangs from her forehead. "No helicopter blades, baby," I whispered so low that she couldn't hear. A little louder I said, "That will go away when you sleep. If you need anything, the light switch is right in front of your nose and the bathroom is the next door on the left."

She didn't reply or move. I was afraid she'd already fallen asleep without hearing the most important information when one was drunk and sick. As much as I adored this girl, I'd

ANNA KATMORE

rather she didn't throw up in my bed. "Did you hear me?"

Her mouth curved into a strained grin. "Light, nose. Toilet, left. Gotcha." She even gave me a thumbs-up, which reassured me.

I rose from the floor, but just when I went to walk away, she said my name. "Hunter?"

Hunkering down again, I leaned my forearms on the mattress. "Hm?"

She dragged a deep sigh. "Sorry about the pool game."

Yeah, I know you are. But I'm not. The way our gazes had met across that table was special. Way too intimate to be brushed off as harmless flirting. I let my glance move around me, scanning the familiar things in my room, then I looked back at her, the one thing that was totally unfamiliar in here. She made everything complete for me.

Gently, so as not to wake her up again, I stroked her warm cheek with the back of my fingers. "Sleep tight, princess."

CHAPTER 6

WITH MY THOUGHTS continuously drifting back to my room and the person who lay in there now, I went back down to the party. If only it was possible to kick everyone out right now, end the night early, and return to Lisa. I wouldn't take advantage of her drunkenness. I wouldn't put any moves on her. The only thing I would do was sit by her side all night and look at her beautiful face.

But then I'd gotten so much out of this night already. We'd flirted and she'd hugged me when I carried her upstairs. She'd told me that I smelled good. Jeez, I was a seriously lucky guy tonight.

When I sauntered back into the poolroom without any drinks, the boys wanted to know where I had been so long. I told them I had to take care of a drunken guest, but I didn't let slip who it was or where I had taken her. Justin was the only exception. I filled him in on everything once the two of us were hanging out in front of the house to cool off after a couple more beers.

Tony came out with Chloe tucked under his arm. "Cool party, Hunter," he told me. "We're off. Do you think I should take Lisa home with me?"

"Nah, let her sleep. She's all right up there. I don't think being woken up now and riding in a car is what she needs or wants."

He nodded, and Chloe seemed more than relieved about his decision to leave Lisa with me. And so was I. When the two left, Justin clinked his bottle against mine and flashed a grin so typical of the Andrews boys. "Seems like this is your lucky night. Why are you not upstairs?"

I took a swig, wondering the same thing. "Because I'm a gentleman."

Justin laughed at that, and I swallowed the rest of the beer in one go. The truth was that I was probably an idiot. And I hated not being with Lisa right now.

The party went on for a couple more hours but ended abruptly when Veronica Malloy threw up on the floor in the hall. Her friends helped me clean up the mess—or maybe they did all the work because by that time I could hardly keep myself upright. Beer, in combination with Claudia's wine cooler, was a very bad thing. But heck, the strawberries were a tasty addition.

When everybody had left, I dragged myself upstairs and into my room. The door slammed shut behind me. I didn't care about being loud, because my mom and dad were still out, and I was the only one in this big, dark house. Or maybe not. Usually, I found some friends in my place in the morning who hadn't made it home after the party. In the silence, my ears still rang from the loud music, and my head felt like a truck had run over it.

"Hunter?"

Holy shit! I nearly jumped out of my skin. There was someone in my room. The voice sounded familiar, and if my head didn't hurt so badly, I probably would have recognized it in the first instant. Now I tried to focus on the girl sitting on my bed in the darkened room. Lisa? Memories came back in a blurred vision. Good memories.

"You're still here?" I drawled, unable to believe my luck. Unbuttoning my shirt, I kicked my shoes into the corner and flung the shirt on top of them.

"Where is *here* exactly? And why are you undressing?" She sounded very uncomfortable as she rubbed her temples.

"Well, for one, this is my room. And second, that thing you're lying on is my bed. Since I don't usually sleep in clothes, I figured I'd just take them off." Duh.

"Is the party over?"

No, baby, the party begins now. I sneered at the beautiful creature waiting for me just a few feet away. But then I realized she probably meant the *previous* party, and my shoulders slumped. "Someone puked on the floor. Yeah. Party's over." And here I stood, totally regretting that I'd had way too much to drink tonight. I should have stayed sober to enjoy this moment without a subway tunneling through my brain. "I swear, next time Claudia brings her strawberry soda, I'm going to kick a girl's butt for the first time in my life. Harmless, my ass."

Lisa groaned. "What time is it?"

"Three."

"A.m.?"

No need to get hysterical. "It's dark outside. Of course it's a.m."

Suddenly, she was out of my bed and on the floor, crawling around. It happened so fast, I could only stay rigid and watch.

"Where are my shoes?" she croaked, patting the floor.

What did she need shoes for? I wanted to tell her to get back into that bed and just snuggle up to me like she'd done when I carried her in. But she didn't look like she wanted that when she got to her feet again.

"What are you doing?"

"Going home!"

"Whoa." Not going to happen. I had to do something to stop her from leaving. We weren't done with each other. I wanted more cuddling! *Think fast. Make her stay.* While thinking itself was hard enough, coming up with something *quickly* was next to impossible. For a start, I placed my hands on her shoulders and pushed her down onto the mattress. "So not a good idea," I told her. "Since we already agreed that it's the dead of night...and you're sixteen...and drunk—"

"Drunk? *No.*"

All right, she was in denial, which was totally fine with me, because I was way past that stage and knew what was really going on. "Whatever. I can't let you do that."

"Do what?"

Yeah, what? "Walk alone."

She frowned. "You want to come with me?"

Hell yes! But not tonight. Because she would only send me home, and I'd be down on my luck. I sat down next to her and tried to focus on her eyes that gleamed nicely in the moonlight shimmering through the window. "It's a mile and a half to your house. That's three for me to walk. I'm positive I won't make that tonight. So if you really want to go home, I'll have to drive you. But right now, I'd rather not." I was drunk, but fortunately I wasn't an idiot.

"So what do I do now?" She looked every bit helpless and lovely.

"I'd say lay back. Sleep. And worry about everything tomorrow."

"What about you?"

I will lay back, won't sleep, and will stare at you until the morning. If she let me sleep next to her, that was. But how to convince her? "The floor is hard. And I'm beat. There's room for two in that bed..."

She looked at me for an intense second, then she suddenly dropped back onto the pillow without another word. Either she was just weird, or she was getting sick. However, the fact that she didn't say I had to sleep on the floor lifted my spirit. "Good choice, Matthews," I mumbled and settled down beside her.

Right then, I was aware of every inch of her that touched me. Her left fist was curled under her chin and pressed against my shoulder, our legs touched the entire length, and if I moved

ANNA KATMORE

my arm just a little, I'd be holding her hand. *Oh my freaking goodness.* It would take so little to roll on top of her and kiss her thoroughly.

I took a deep, steadying breath and wondered if she had the tiniest idea of how much effort it cost an eighteen-year-old guy to rein in so much testosterone. But I did—for now. And only because I wanted to be fully aware of all my senses when I kissed Lisa Matthews.

Tilting my head to her side, I let her know through a smirk exactly how I felt. Then I growled, "I swear you're safe with me for the next three to six hours. I can't make promises for any time after that, though."

I wasn't sure if she was aware of the small smile that just slipped to her lips. She gazed into my eyes for a moment longer, then her pretty eyes closed. It didn't take long until her breathing became even, evidence of her being asleep.

Hard to say how much longer I studied her that night. I lost my sense of time. But when I couldn't hold my eyes open any longer, I was positive that every little detail of her beautiful face was etched into my memory. The three freckles on the tip of her nose, the fact that the right curve of her upper lip was just a tad higher than the left, her long lashes that rested on her downy skin when her eyes were closed. She smelled like the roses in our garden, and her hair felt like fine sand running through my fingers.

I fell asleep with one thought. This girl was mine. She just didn't know it yet.

The next thing I knew I lay on my back in what seemed to be my bed, and someone's eyes were fixed on me. My arm was draped over my eyes, so I couldn't see, but the awareness ran from the back of my neck down to the very tips of my toes.

However long it had been, this wasn't the first time I woke up with a girl in my bed. But for once, I had no memory whatsoever of what had happened last night, and who I had taken up to my room with me. It was a weird feeling, especially since we seemed to have taken on quite an entangled position from what I could tell.

"I can feel you staring at me," I said, without turning or taking my arm away from my eyes. The warm hand that had rested on my chest snapped away. "I only hope you're a girl and not one of the drunken guys." I reached down to the leg that was draped over my hip. Wow, that leg was naked and satiny soft. "Yep, definitely female."

I wondered how much more naked skin I would find if I ran my palm upwards. Unfortunately, I didn't get very far, because the girl's hand caught mine in a tight grip and held it in place.

"Move another inch, Hunter, and you're a dead man."

Could someone stab me in the eye right now, please, so I know I'm not dreaming? It was the most wonderful sound to wake up to, and totally surreal to hear it in my room, especially

ANNA KATMORE

next to my ear when I was lying in my bed. I laughed softly. "Matthews?"

Oh glorious morning, so much for getting Lisa into my bed before the *week* was over.

She didn't reply, but then she didn't have to. I knew it was her, could tell by her sweet scent. Our hands were still joined on her thigh, and it didn't seem like she was going to let go of me any time soon.

It was time to open my eyes and take a peek at what I'd done last night. Dropping my arm to the pillow above my head, I turned toward her and instantly took in that she was fully dressed, even though I only seemed to be wearing my jeans. I most definitely hadn't slept with her, which I was unspeakably glad of, because I couldn't remember a thing. But that didn't mean she had to be so abrasive. "Tell me, Matthews. Why do I have you in my bed, when I'm not allowed to touch you?"

She looked at me for a stunned second, then her face crinkled to a grimace. "I didn't know there were strawberries in the soda."

Right. And that meant what? "Come again?"

"Someone was getting me berry soda all evening." Her voice didn't sound really steady, and her gaze kept drifting down to her naked thigh, which I still had my hand on. "I didn't realize it was the wine cooler you meant when you said—
"

"Not to touch the strawberries." Heck, now I remembered. Claudia's wine cooler was the reason Lisa lay in my bed, with her sexy calf resting on my groin. Unfortunately, it was also the reason I couldn't remember much of the previous night. "Damn, I told her not to punch it too much," I muttered. Then I studied Lisa's face for a sign that I should be worried this morning. "Sorry, I don't remember much of the night after I carried you up here. Am I in trouble?"

"As far as I remember you were pretty drunk yourself. So I was quite safe from you."

That she had been. But I was clear in my head now, and having her laying half on top of me gave me pretty cool, maybe X-rated thoughts. Her smooth skin tempted me to stroke and explore, and I started to run my thumb in small circles over her thigh. "I'm afraid my time of numb indifference is over. So, unless you're up for some trouble *now*, would you mind moving your leg?"

Her eyes grew wide at that, and she clearly didn't know how to respond.

"What?" I gave her a tentative smirk. "You know you're not the ugliest girl in the world."

For some reason, that must not have gone down so well with her, because the next thing I knew, she'd pushed aside my bent leg, with which I'd trapped hers in place, and rushed out of my bed. She was crazy, or maybe just not used to a hangover, but it was clear she'd suffer a head-rush any second, and I didn't want her to black out in my room. I got up with her and, before she had a chance to fall, I cupped her elbows.

She took a second to steady, then she looked up at my

face.

"Feel better?" I asked.

"Not really." She slipped out of my hold and grabbed her shoes from the end of the bed where I had put them last night, if I remembered it right.

I gave her a minute to put them on then headed downstairs, knowing she'd follow me. The tiled floor felt cold against my bare feet. I needed that now to settle down my boiling blood.

"Hey, Hunter," someone called from the hall as we came down the stairs.

"Morning, Chris," I said back and found him sprawled on a sofa. His look when he realized who was trotting down after me was hilarious.

As we reached the bottom of the stairs, Lisa wanted to take a turn for the front door, but I couldn't let her slip out like that. Not without a goodbye and some advice on dealing with a hangover. Taking her hand, I pulled her into the kitchen where I gave her a water bottle with an aspirin dissolving in it.

Standing rigid in the middle of the room, she sniffed the water but didn't drink.

"Why so skeptical, Matthews? It will ease your headache," I said as I leaned against the counter and took a swig of my own sobering drink.

The sip she took then would hardly have been enough to drown an ant.

"You don't trust me?"

"How could I?" she answered. "I woke up with a hangover from soda and with an equally drunk person sleeping next to me half of the night."

Ouch. "Yeah, sorry about that. I don't usually get drunk at my own parties." Not from beer, anyway. "And believe me I'm going to give Claudia an earful for messing with the wine cooler." I rubbed the back of my neck. "Look, as long as you keep hydrated today, you'll be fine."

She massaged her temples, and didn't look one bit like she believed the headache would ever go away again. "It feels like someone installed a construction site in my head."

"Oh yeah, I know the feeling." It was like I invented it. But the aspirin usually worked wonders. "If you give me a minute to shower, I'll drive you home."

"No!" she blurted and shocked the hell out of me. Or maybe it was just disappointment, because she made it sound like she couldn't get away from me fast enough. At the same time, her face scrunched up, and she winced. Then she said in a softer tone, "No thanks. I'll be happy to take the walk and sober up before seeing my parents. My mom will freak out."

Oh, okay. That I could understand. "Suit yourself. Want my sunglasses?" I added as I walked her to the door.

"Why would I want your sunglasses?" She pulled the door open, and with the first sunrays streaming in, she flinched back and knocked straight into my chest.

Ah hell, I could do that all day. And unless I was totally mistaken, she enjoyed the brief body contact, too. "I know you so want 'em," I purred into her ear with every intention of seducing her back into my room. But if she didn't trust me enough to drink what I served her, she'd never come upstairs with me sober. I just had to work a little harder to make her trust me. And tomorrow I'd get the first real chance during our personal training.

I gave her my shades, which I'd left on the shelf next to the coatrack yesterday when I'd come in after training, and Lisa put them on before she left my house without saying goodbye.

"Matthews," I called after her. She didn't really think she'd get away that easily, did she? "We'll start your training tomorrow morning. Be up and ready at five. I'll pick you up."

And just so she didn't get a chance to change her mind or talk herself out of our date, I cast her a last smile then closed the door on her stunned face.

Hell no, I wouldn't let her get off and go back on her word.

Back in the hall, I made Chris help me clean up what my mom hadn't already done this morning. We moved the furniture back into place and rolled out the carpets. As we carried the boxes of empty beer bottles into the garage, he seemed to finally wake up fully.

"So that's it?" he said with the edge of surprise in his voice. "You already had the chick in your bed?"

"What? Now you doubt me? Yesterday you sounded way different, dude." Stacking the boxes in the far corner, I let loose a brilliant smirk. "But it's not really what it looks like. I didn't touch her at all." I reconsidered. "Or if I did, I don't remember."

"Ah, I never thought I'd say this, but it's those girls that make you *wait* who are totally worth their salt."

Wait, whine, beg on my knees—Lisa could have all of that from me. She only had to snap her fingers. Of course, I would never let her know that. She'd only be introduced to the art of subtle seduction. And I liked how one thing had led to another these past few days.

Later that day, Alex sent me a text message saying that a few guys from the team were meeting at the beach. It was mid-August, the perfect season for surfing. I met up with them at three in the afternoon, and when I saw Mitchell pulling up in his parents' car, a brief flicker of hope that he might have brought Lisa struck me motionless. Unfortunately, it was a blonde and not a brunette climbing out with him.

Alex and I took a few rides on nice waves, seeing who was the better surfer today. When the girls tiptoed into the sea, I made an exit, though, shook out my wet hair, and slumped down next to Mitchell. He pretended to be sunbathing when in fact he was watching Chloe in the water through his opaque sunglasses.

"Things are cool between you and Summers?" I asked.

"Absolutely."

"I'm surprised you didn't bring Lisa. The girls could be *playing* in the water together," I mocked him and put my cap on over my wet hair. "Does she know we're hanging out here?"

"She knows," he replied and looked at me for the first time, taking off his glasses.

Wow, he didn't look happy all of a sudden. That made me abandon my taunting grin. "What's up?"

"I asked her to come, but she can't. Her mom grounded her for the rest of the week. And then Liz was pissed because, one, she thinks I forgot her at your place, and two, because Chloe is here with us, and she's not."

"Ouch."

"Yeah, it sucks *majorly*." Tony put the glasses on again to watch some more of a nearly naked Chloe, and it brightened his mood in an instant. "Liz also said you weren't your usual self this morning."

"*What*?"

A shit-eating grin appeared on his lips again. "She said you behaved like a perfect gentleman. I didn't think you'd be able to keep it together when a girl was sleeping in your bed and you're drunk to boot."

I laughed about that. "So my usual self is a horny dickhead who'd grab any chance he got to make out with a girl?"

"Sounds about right."

I mirrored Mitchell's smirk. "Guilty." Even if that self was now in the past. But it was nice to know Lisa thought of me as a gentleman. Meant I did *something* right last night. "What are you going to do about her being pissed at you?"

Tony shrugged. "Dunno. Make it up to her somehow. Maybe drop in and watch some movies with her since she can't go out."

"Are you going to tell her about Chloe?"

"Eventually. I don't have a choice." He grabbed a handful of sand and let it run through his fingers. "But not while she's angry with me. She'll never *ever* speak to me again if I screw this up."

I rolled onto my stomach, enjoying the warm sun on my back. "Dude, you better tell her fast. I think she'll hate you more if she hears it from someone else." That Mitchell had brought Chloe here today made things a little more obvious. The guys on the team would be talking, even if they didn't mean to hurt anyone.

"I'll get it sorted out with her in the next few days," Tony said, but the sigh he heaved sounded like he dreaded nothing more than that little chat with his best friend.

I smoothed out the beach towel beneath me, folded my arms on the ground, and rested my chin in the crook of my elbow, intending to catch up on some missed sleep. Tony had different plans. I heard him roll to his front, too, and let go of a long sigh, so I opened my eyes again.

"Do you think Lisa already suspects something?" he asked me.

"Seriously, Mitchell, if she doesn't, she must be blind. But you know, when you're in love, there's this denial button you just switch on, and everything is good for a while."

"You saying she doesn't want to believe it?"

"I believe she could see you fool around with Summers in

the water and kiss, and it would only take one word from you to convince her you had to give Chloe mouth to mouth resuscitation." As my own words sank in and made total sense, even I started to dread their little chat. Lisa hurting was the last thing I wanted. "Anyway, how do you think this will work out? I mean, once you dump the bomb on her. You can't have a relationship triangle. The girls hate each other. They'll always be jealous of one another."

"I'll make it work. Somehow." Now he sounded like a sullen child that hadn't gotten the toy he'd seen in a shop window.

"Tony, listen to me, because I'm your friend. And right now you can't even begin to understand how *good* a friend I am for telling you this. You can't have the both of them. And in the long run, Lisa Matthews is the better choice for you. One with a future."

Resting on his elbows, Tony laced his fingers in the sand and let his head hang. "I told you that it'll never be like that between Liz and me."

Fuck, I hated myself for saying this. "If you don't want to lose her, you have to think about making her your girlfriend. Because: She. Loves. You. And I've known you long enough to see that you do, too." I growled, clamping my teeth together. "And now go away. I want to sleep." And not totally destroy my flickering chance with Lisa.

But then I'd probably done the right thing. If there would ever be an *us* for Lisa and me, I wanted to be the only one in her thoughts, not fighting against something that wouldn't happen for her, anyway. They needed to get this thing straight between them or else I'd be the one hurting in the end, when they both realized later they were meant for each other. I didn't think I would survive getting myself lost in Lisa and then losing her to someone else.

So however things developed between us, I wouldn't kiss her until she knew the truth about Mitchell and Summers.

CHAPTER 7

BEFORE I WENT to bed that night, I set the alarm on my phone to four thirty. That would give me enough time to dress and get over to Lisa's house before five. Then I stripped down to my boxers, turned off the light, and climbed into my bed. The window was wide open, and I could hear the crickets in our garden. It wasn't their noise that kept me from sleeping, it was thinking about who had slept next to me in this bed last night.

I had never thought it possible that a couple of days could make such a difference. Suddenly, this bed felt way too big to sleep in alone.

Scooting back to lean against the headboard, I switched my nightstand light on and hugged a pillow to my chest. With my chin pressed into the feathers, I scanned the familiar room around me. Though nothing in here had changed in the previous two years, it now felt empty. Something was missing. A pair of apple-green eyes staring at me. The sound of Lisa's even breaths in the dark.

I wanted her back with me. I wanted to be the first thing she thought of in the morning and the last to tell her good night. I wanted all of her. And goddammit, I was so tired of waiting.

With the light turned off again, I remained sitting in my bed for a long while. In fact, I must have fallen asleep that way, because when the alarm went off in the early morning hours, I found myself curled in a strange position against the headboard, still hugging the pillow. I groaned and got up, rubbing the nasty kink in my neck.

A few stretches and push-ups helped ease the stiffness. Slipping on a black tee and shorts, I felt the rush of excitement coming over me. While I had endured most of the summer without seeing Lisa, the past twenty-four hours without her had been torture.

I washed my face, brushed my teeth, and slipped on my sneakers, then I headed downstairs and out to my car. From hanging out at Mitchell's place for years, I knew where Lisa lived.

I didn't know if she was ready to go or still asleep, and if I had to wake her, how I would go about it, since it wasn't really an option to ring the bell at five in the morning. Mitchell shouldn't see my car in front of her house if he got up early, so I parked two houses down then walked back up.

Everything was silent, the street as well as her house. No light shone from any room. In the dark, I walked around the house, wondering what to do. Maybe I should just throw a pebble at one of the upstairs windows. But if that was her parents' bedroom, I might get into trouble. Brilliant.

Above a small shed beside the house, the window to one room was open. The glass didn't reflected much, but a desk and

ANNA KATMORE

a wardrobe. Could be the room of any teenager. Maybe she'd left it open because she knew I was coming? It was the best chance I'd get, so I decided to try.

"Matthews," I called to her in what happened to be a little more than a whisper—more a suppressed shout. Nothing happened for a minute, so I tried again, just a little louder than before. This time it took about ten seconds until my very own Juliet appeared in the window. My heart knocked its approval when I saw her. First, because I had really, really missed her. And second, because I'd picked the right window and not that of an angry father who'd come after me with a shotgun for seducing his daughter.

She looked sleepy and surprised to see me here.

"Hi," I said. "You don't look like you're ready to go."

Lisa leaned over the sill, her long hair slipping from her shoulders and hanging down. "How did you know this was my window?"

"I didn't. It was trial and error."

Her face paled in the dark. "How many windows have you tried?"

I laughed and gave her the truth. "Yours."

Something was going on inside her head. I couldn't tell what, but some very interesting emotions played out in her eyes then. Shock, fascination, happiness, then shock again. All the time, she didn't say anything.

"Are you coming?" I demanded.

"I can't. I'm grounded," she whispered back.

"For sleeping with me?"

That made her smile, even though she tried to hide it. *Baby, you failed.*

"For not sleeping in my own bed," was what she answered.

"How long are you grounded?"

"Until Sunday. But I can come to the practices."

"At least there's that." I would have hated not to see her there when she was, at long last, on my team. But I wanted to train with her now, too. There had to be a way to get her out of that room without her parents finding out. Scanning the garden, the tree, and the shed, I had an idea. "What time do you usually get up in the morning?"

She narrowed her eyes. "I don't know. Eight, nine, sometimes later."

"So we have at least three hours until someone will expect you downstairs." That was enough time to get her out, do some running, and get her in again. And I wouldn't waste one minute of that precious time with her. With a flick of my head, I motioned for her to get moving. "Come out."

"What?" she gasped.

"Get dressed and climb to the roof of the shed. I'll help you down."

"You're crazy."

I smirked. "*You* are a coward."

"I'm not!"

"Prove it."

She bit her bottom lip, looking a bit wary, in need of a

little push. "So?" I prompted.

"Fine. Give me a minute."

Hell, yeah! I squeezed my eyes shut for a moment, keeping a leash on my delight. While Lisa disappeared into her room again, I leaned against the tree and spied through the window, trying to see what was going on up there. Unfortunately, I saw nothing but a shadow.

I stepped closer to the shed when she reappeared and started climbing out the window. She looked scared and clumsy, definitely not a fan of acrobatic moves. After a minute, she'd made it down to the roof of the shed.

"Good," I encouraged her. "Now hang onto that branch, and I'll get you down."

Lisa turned wide eyes to me, all but calling me insane for even suggesting it. "I'll break my neck if I fall."

She would hurt her ass if she fell. Maybe. However, I didn't intend to let her get hurt. "I won't let you fall. Promise."

It amazed me how quickly she trusted me this time, because without further discussion, she grabbed the nearest branch and stepped off the wooden roof. She probably hated that I heard her frightened whimper, but I found it sexy as hell.

As she hung on that tree like a sheet on the clothesline, my gaze ran up and down her body. What I did next would certainly be the highlight of my day, and I intended to savor it to the full. Stepping so close that I could touch her, I placed my hands at the back of her calves then moved them upward over her thighs, until I had a good grip right beneath her butt. All her muscles tightened at my touch.

I had to unstick my tongue from the roof of my mouth before I could speak again. "I have you. Let go."

"*What*?"

What did she think we were doing here? Did she want to hang from that tree for the rest of the day? "Let go of the branch, Matthews," I said, laughing. "*Now.*"

After some moaning and unintelligible cussing, she let go of the branch, and the weight of a kitten came down on me. Panicking, she clutched at my shoulders, and I found myself trapped in her gorgeous green eyes. Finally, I eased my grip on her legs and let her slide down my body. Holy shit, that move turned me on like nothing ever had. When her feet touched the ground, I wasn't ready to let her go. With my arms wrapped around her in a tight embrace, I inhaled her scent and soaked in the warmth of her body.

A smile tugged at my lips. "Hi."

With her palms pressed against my chest, she shivered. That made me feel good because it wasn't the least bit cold this morning, so *I* had to be the reason for her trembles. It was sweet how she struggled to hide that fact behind a calm expression as she stepped out of my hug.

"Can we go?" I asked, still smiling.

"Where to?"

"The beach."

She gulped, probably because it was quite a distance, but she nodded anyway like a brave kitten. We started off together, and I settled for a seriously slow pace, so she wouldn't collapse after a couple hundred yards.

I was used to running in the morning on weekends and usually enjoyed it because it was the only time of the day where everything was really quiet and peaceful. But with Lisa by my side it was twice as nice.

We jogged down a few streets with houses that all looked alike as dawn broke. Lisa did great—meaning she hadn't resigned yet. But I didn't like the silence between us and asked, "So your parents got angry because you didn't get home Saturday night?"

"No," she pushed out between erratic breaths. "My parents thought I crashed at Tony's. Which is fine with them."

What the hell—she'd slept at Mitchell's house? I almost tripped over my own feet. The bastard had never said a word about that. "You do that often?"

Lisa cut me a curious glance. "You sound like you disapprove."

Of course I did! I scowled at her, but didn't answer as long as I felt this invisible fist clenching my stomach. Only when we got closer to the ocean and the sound of crashing waves drifted to us did I manage to sound normal again. "So why the grounding?"

She rubbed a forearm over her sweaty forehead. "My mom saw my red eyes and figured I'd been drinking." Then she cussed, which made me arch a brow at her. "I forgot your sunglasses."

"No worries." I had forgotten about them, too. "You can give them to me tomorrow before practice."

She nodded, and it was clear that the little distance we'd run so far had troubled her a lot more than me. She sounded like a pair of bellows. As soon as we reached the beach, Lisa slumped to the sand as though she had no life left in her anymore.

That was not part of the plan. I stood over her, hands on my hips, and gazed at her reddened face. "What are you doing?"

"Dying."

I liked how she made me chuckle with such simple things. "No, you're not. Get up, we're not done."

"*I* am," she protested. "But don't mind me. You just go on. I'm sure in a few hours someone will come and scrape me off the pavement." She waved a dismissive hand. "Dig me out of the sand. Whatever."

Laughing, I squatted down and started to untie her shoes for what was coming next. We weren't done yet.

"Hey, what the heck—" She pulled her leg away. "You don't steal from a dying person."

I surrendered, lifting my hands, palms up. "Fine, then take them off yourself."

"What?" Her mouth sagged open as she propped up on her elbows in the sand and looked at me with wide eyes. "Why?" Then her gaze moved to the sea and her lips spread in a hopeful grin. "We're going to take a swim now to cool off after all that training?"

"Nope," I said, though she put a very beguiling thought in my head right then. I could be swayed to some fooling around in the water with her. But that would be too much of a temptation. Kisses came along with such nonsense. And I had sworn to myself that I wouldn't do that until she knew the truth about Mitchell. After a longing glance at the sea, I faced her again and said with a firm voice that wouldn't get me into trouble, "The little run was only warm-up. The training begins here."

All color disappeared from her face. "You can't be serious."

"What are you willing to bet on it?"

She grimaced and sighed, but I'd figured out by now that my word counted to her, and she slipped her shoes off to hide them with mine by the rocks. I wondered if it was just the team captain she saw in me, or if she wanted to make a good impression because she saw me, the nice guy.

Only a few minutes later, she made it clear she didn't see me as a nice guy when she shot me a look filled with loathing. "Do your parents know about this sadistic side of yours?"

I remembered the first time I'd run on the beach for training. Her calves probably hurt like mad. But she had to get through this. We wanted to turn her into a kick-ass soccer player. I tugged gently at her high ponytail. "What can I say? You bring out my best side."

"Ah, great. I feel so special now." Lisa shoved my shoulder, and I laughed as I struggled to steady myself with my feet sinking into the soft sand. "How far are we going?" she demanded.

"I never ran this route before, but I guess it's about a half-mile. You know the houses at Misty Beach?"

"Your parents own a house down there?"

"Yep." It was a nice little thing compared to the mansion we lived in, and I really liked to come out here after training on weekends and study or read on the wraparound veranda. My dad had set up a porch swing for Rachel and me when we were kids, and it was the perfect place to relax and enjoy a warm summer day.

We still had a way to go, and when Misty Beach finally came into view, I thought Lisa couldn't endure another step. She licked her lips, and her lungs made a weird, gasping sound. "I swear I'm going to drink up the ocean," she cried.

"Chin up, Matthews. We're almost there." I grabbed her upper arm when she stumbled and didn't let her stop just yet, dragging her along with me the last few yards. As I led her up to our bungalow, her face lit up, seriously proud of herself. And I was, too.

There was always a set of keys in the potted plant on the broad railing of the porch. I fished them out and let us in. The door slammed shut behind us.

While Lisa stood rooted in the living room, her gaze traveling over the couch, wide-screen TV, and especially over the bookshelf, I headed into the sun-infused kitchen. From the fridge, I grabbed two bottles of water and tossed one at Lisa.

ANNA KATMORE

She guzzled the water down as if she came equipped with a camel hump, then wiped her lips with the back of her hand. "So, great tormentor, why did we run on the beach? Was it just for your personal pleasure of seeing me suffer?"

My personal pleasure would be to see her strip naked right now. Rolling my eyes at her, I cracked a smile. "Why do you think so badly of me?"

"I don't know." She left her spot on the wall and leaned her delicious butt against the backrest of the couch. As she folded her arms over her chest, it gave her words that sweet edge of sarcasm. "Maybe because I lost my lungs somewhere on the way here? Or because my legs are on fire?"

"Oh, come on now," I teased her. "We jogged over two miles and you're still standing. That's great. And running in the sand will strengthen your legs a lot better than the pavement. Since we only run on grass at soccer, you need to get used to the additional—"

"Torture?"

Smart-ass. "Exactly." I walked toward her and gently swiped her sweaty bangs out of her eyes. Every time I touched her, I could think about nothing else than a first, tender kiss. Something in her look told me she was becoming aware of it, too. Breaking our locked gazes, I took the empty bottle out of her hands and tossed it along with mine into the trash can. Then I stiffened at the sound of footsteps on the porch.

Shit. That was my mom.

My glance skidded to the door then back at Lisa. Not a

good moment to have her here. Lisa seemed equally shocked, but maybe just because I was sort of panicking right in front of her. There wasn't time for an explanation. As my mom's key rattled in the lock, I started toward Lisa and tried not to hurt her as I knocked her backward over the couch. We landed on the cushions together, then I rolled to the side and pulled her down to the hard wooden floor with me, out of my mom's sight. Lisa landing on top of me was, hands down, the summit of my dreams, but it also pushed all the air out of my lungs.

As she scowled down at me, I could feel her warm breath on my face. Something in her expression softened for a millisecond. Like she was surprised by what she saw there in my eyes.

"Who is it?" she hissed, and her gaze turned annoyed once again.

"Can only be my mom," I whispered back and suppressed a moan, then shoved her off of me. It was safer for both of us if she didn't stay on top of me in this unbelievable *turn-me-on* position. I squeezed her in between the couch and me and placed one hand over her mouth to keep her silent while my mom carried several boxes into the kitchen. "She's stocking the fridge."

As my lips brushed against her ear, Lisa closed her eyes. Her warm breath caressed the back of my hand. Enjoying it, was she? So what the hell was stopping me from kissing around her ear a little just to make her sigh like that again? Ah right, noise drifting from behind the couch did.

A few seconds later, Lisa pulled my hand away from her lips. "Why are we hiding here?"

Because things like girls were a complicated issue between my folks and me. "My parents don't like me bringing random girls to this place. Unless you want to be introduced as my girlfriend, I suggest you stay down."

She didn't move. Okay, apparently being introduced as my girlfriend wasn't her goal, however much it was mine. But I really didn't want to answer questions from my mom, so I appreciated Lisa's silent agreement.

It didn't take long for my mom to finish and leave the bungalow. Just to be sure, I waited another minute before I got to my feet.

Lisa breathed a relieved sigh. She wouldn't take my hand when I offered to help her up, but remained lying, legs bent, feet on the floor, and folded her arms behind her head. "You sure your dad isn't on his way, too?"

"Yes, I'm sure." Silly little girl. "He never comes here during the week." Ignoring her belligerent behavior, I reached down for her hand and pulled. "Get up."

Rising, she patted invisible dust off her butt. "Next time you feel the need to knock me over, I'd appreciate a little warning first."

If that's all it would take to drag her down with me... "Sure thing!"

I went to the bathroom in the back of the house, right next to my bedroom, and fetched a fresh towel from the shelf.

Walking back to the front, I wiped my face and neck with it then tossed it at Lisa so she could towel off, too.

She caught it, then looked at the terry cloth with a wry face. "Ew."

Ew? Seriously? I stopped, turning to her, about to tell her that she was now a soccer player, not running for Miss California.

But her snappy tongue was faster than mine. "I don't know how a little running together got us to that level of intimacy."

It just did. Deal with it. She got my arching of a brow as an answer and, ignoring her grimace, I walked out on the porch and slumped down on the swing. It took only half a minute for her to follow me, and hey, she was rubbing her neck with my used towel.

She tossed it back at me with a hard thrust. I caught it before the bundle smacked me in the face.

"Let's go back," she muttered.

Already? I didn't want to just yet. "Are we in a hurry, Matthews?"

She looked around uncomfortably, clearly not in the mood to hang out on the swing, then decided to park her sexy body against the post next to the wooden steps that led down to the beach. "Not really. But I won't stay in a place where I have to sign a marriage license to be welcome," she snapped.

Was she still scared of my mom? "She won't come back."

"I don't care." She cast me a glare that spelled out, *Come back with me or drop dead.*

"Fair enough. Let me just get the ball, then we can go." I stood and walked back to my room for the soccer ball I kept there in case some friends came down here with me and we wanted to play on the beach. I stuffed it into a backpack together with a bottle of water and the towel that lay on the swing.

Shouldering the load, I dumped the keys back into the potted plant and ushered Lisa down the steps. She didn't look like she could cope with running another couple of miles, so we ambled back instead.

The sky cleared from rosy to blue, and it was nice to walk barefoot in the sand, with the water brushing around my ankles and my girl strolling beside me. I wanted to reach out and take her hand, oh so terribly much. But she seemed a little stiff since we'd left the beach house, so I didn't dare push my luck.

"Why did you bring the ball?" she asked after a while of silent walking.

"You need to practice kicking and catching. The beach is perfect for that."

We reached the rocks where we'd hidden our shoes and put them on. Then I told her to stay put while I jogged some thirty feet back and got the ball out from my backpack. "I want you to stop the ball," I shouted at her before I kicked.

But all she did was shriek and catch the ball to her chest with her arms. What the heck— "This is soccer. You're not supposed to use your hands," I told her. "Kick it back."

She cast me a wary look and kicked the ball back at me. Not only did she raise a sandstorm with it, but the ball also missed me by ten feet. The girl was going to need quite a bit of coaching. But I was totally up to it. I jogged to the ball and kicked hard.

Lisa caught it again.

I cut a glance to the sky and rubbed my palms over my face. "No hands, Matthews!"

We shot back and forth a third time, and now she simply stepped aside and let the ball race past her. She couldn't be serious.

"What was that?" I shouted as I jogged over to her.

"You said no hands," Lisa snapped. "Want me to catch it with my teeth or what?"

"I strongly suggest you don't do that." I grimace. "During a game you will have to stop the ball. But you're not allowed to use your hands. So you use your body to block it. Your shoulders, or head, but mostly your chest."

"Aha. There's only one problem with that." She cupped her boobs with both hands. "I've got these!"

I couldn't believe she just did that. A girl should *never* touch her own boobs when a guy is present...unless she wants to strike him dumb and ruin any chance of ordinary conversation for him. I gulped, as my mouth and throat went dry, unable to look at anything other than the nice handful she held.

She let go of her jugs and said shit to me I couldn't

understand, but I guessed it had to do with the fact that she didn't like me staring at her when drool was coming out of my mouth. Slowly and with a smirk, I tore my gaze away from that delicious part of her body and looked at her red face.

"Enough training for one morning." Her croak betrayed her, and I happened to really enjoy that. She looked away, digging her toe into the sand. "I want to be back before my mom finds out I'm gone."

That was fine with me. But I didn't let her off the first training day so easily. After some protesting, she finally agreed that we'd run at least half the way back then walk the rest to cool down. As we reached her house, she suddenly pulled me across the street and behind a tree. I followed like a well-trained puppy, totally ready to make out with her in that hiding place. But she wasn't even thinking about it.

With her back pressed against the trunk, she leaned carefully to the side and spied around the tree. When she snapped back into an upright position, she glanced at the sky and whined, "I'm so screwed."

I looked around the tree, too. Okay, so somebody was walking around in a room downstairs, and that room was close to the front door. Could be worse. I nudged her chin with the knuckle of my finger and made her look at me. "Do you always give up that quickly?"

"Apparently, *you* don't," she retorted. "So what do you suggest?"

Easy. "We get you inside the same way we got you out."

Lisa narrowed her eyes at me. "The window?"

"Exactly."

"Tony has been climbing in and out of there for years. But I don't see how I can do it."

Say that again! My heart refused to take the next beat, and I couldn't help my face turning into an annoyed scowl. "Mitchell has been climbing into your room?"

"Yes. But I need a ladder to get onto the roof of the shed. And as far as I know, we don't have a ladder."

Stop and rewind. Mitchell climbs into her room? "Why?"

"Why what?"

Come on, stay focused, girl! "Why does he climb through your window?"

"Can we please stay focused?"

That's what I'm doing!

"I'm grounded and I need to sneak into my own house," she snarled, not answering my question.

I wanted to growl at her, grab her shoulders, and forbid that Mitchell ever do that again. But she seemed really desperate to get back inside, and I felt bad, seeing her troubled like this. So I swallowed past my irritation and nodded. "All right. Come on." Grabbing a fistful of her white top, I hauled her across the street. No one seemed to be anywhere near a window, so we were safe.

On the other side, she quickly hid behind the shed, scanning the garden for her parents.

I scanned it, too, but for a way to get her upstairs. The tree would work. "I believe Mitchell climbs up there to get onto the roof?"

"Um, yes." Her gaze skated to me. "But you aren't asking me to climb a tree now, are you?"

No, hun, I'm asking you to fly. I suppressed that sarcastic comment, because she looked worried enough, and instead tested the edge of the shed's roof with my weight. As I hung on it, no board cracked, so I guessed we were good to go. "Come here, Matthews."

She watched me as I took a position underneath the roof's edge. "What are you doing?"

"Giving you a lift." Lacing my fingers, I hoped she'd been given a leg up before and knew how this worked.

"No way," she almost screamed, which was funny, because her mother might just have heard that.

"Don't be a baby," I dared her. It had worked this morning when I'd wanted her to climb out, so I was confident it would hit a sensitive spot again. "I already proved I can hold you, remember? Twice."

She looked over her shoulder one last time then came forward and planted her hands on my shoulders, exhaling a deep sigh. Yeah, that was my girl. I went a little lower so we were on eye level to make it easier for her. "Ready?"

Her grip tightened on my shoulders. "Not at all."

"See you tomorrow." I pushed her up, and when she landed flat on her stomach on the roof, I shoved her further up by her feet.

She got on her knees first, then on her feet, and walked over to her open window. At least climbing back inside didn't trouble her. But the look she gave me when she turned around was none too happy. "I don't think we should do this again."

"Why not?"

"I'm dead if my parents catch me."

"They won't."

"What if?"

"Matthews, they won't," I growled, not intending to let her out of our deal. Training with her had been too nice today. "Now shut up and go have a shower."

Her jaw hardened to a frustrated grimace. "Well, I'm not coming tomorrow. There's training with the team anyway. I won't survive two rounds of torture on the same day."

"Yeah. Right." After what I saw of her endurance today, I totally agreed to that. I wanted to spend time with her, not kill her. But the deal was still intact. "Wednesday. Five o'. Be dressed this time. And Matthews—" I smirked at her, just so she got me right. "Don't make me climb up there and fetch you."

Because I sure as hell would go up and carry her out draped over my shoulder if I had to.

CHAPTER 8

BACK IN MY room, I wondered if Mitchell was making good on his promise to hang out with Lisa today. Though it was good for them if they made up, I really disliked the thought of him climbing through her window and lounging on her bed, watching films with her. In fact, it bothered me all day, and I found myself prowling through the house like a restless tiger. Not even playing video games with Justin in the afternoon could take my thoughts off Lisa and Tony. My possessiveness grew and left me in a state where I might have broken all his fingers if he dared to even touch her.

By the evening, I couldn't bear being with myself any longer and decided to give Mitchell a call.

"What's cracking?" he answered the phone.

"Nothing much. Bored as hell. Wanna come play some *Call of Duty*?"

"Sorry, can't. I'm meeting Chloe in twenty."

Pacing my room, I growled, but with my palm placed over the phone so he wouldn't hear me. Then I said, "How did things go with Matthews? You cool now?"

There was a little pause and a weird Tony-sigh. "I guess, but I can't tell for sure."

Now that made me curious. I slumped into my desk chair, stacking my feet on the corner of my bed. "What did you do?"

"Nothing, really. I went over, we watched her favorite movies, and then suddenly she threw me out."

"She did what?" Oh my God, could it get any better?

"She seemed totally distracted all day, which is totally untypical for her when she can watch Hugh Jackman in action."

I took a look at myself in the mirror on the door. A sneer slipped to my lips as I had a pretty good idea of what might have been distracting her.

Tony continued, "Some time in the afternoon she found a lame-ass excuse to make me leave without hurting my feelings."

"But you *are* hurt." No chance of missing that, even over the phone.

"Of course, I am. I mean, she's never done that before. Something's totally off with her recently."

Dipping my head back, I studied the spotlights on the ceiling. "I told you she'd find out what's going on. Maybe that's it. If you don't come clean with her soon, you might only make it worse." And as soon as he did, Lisa would be mine. Dammit, I didn't want to wait any longer.

"Yeah, I know that. So I'll tell her tomorrow after practice. Also because I don't want to sleep with Chloe before I've got things straight with Liz." He gave a bitter laugh. "And Chloe seems to have reached her patience limit where that's concerned."

And here I was trying to talk my friend out of her again,

but this time I swore to myself it would be the very last time. "You still sure about that?" I sighed. "I can just picture how you're going to be single after that one night."

"Totally sure. Chloe's the right one for me." There was a short silence, then he went on, "I know you only mean it in the best way possible, but believe me, she won't dump me."

"All right. You're on your own then, dude. I hope it's worth it for you. See you at practice tomorrow."

I hung up and went to do some needless nonsense just to kill time until it was late enough to go to bed. With the news of Lisa being a bit rattled today hanging in the air, I couldn't wait to see her tomorrow.

Three p.m. Tuesday was a long time coming. While I usually got to practice just in time to start, today I found myself on the ground early, scanning for Lisa. She stood at the middle of the field, waiting for Tony, who was just jogging over to her. I walked up behind her, but he beat me there and said, "Hi, Liz. Are those shades new?"

Ah, so she'd brought my sunglasses. "Nope, they're mine," I said, as I stepped around Lisa and pulled them off her nose. She didn't protest but gifted me with the sweetest smile, which made my day. I didn't fail to notice that not even Tony had gotten such a nice greeting today. And it clearly confused him.

Lisa noticed his puzzled look, too, and quickly explained,

"He gave them to me after the party. Hangover and sunlight—not a good combination."

I remembered the moment she'd knocked into my bare chest because of the blinding light and laughed. Now, with the warm sun on our backs, we walked over to the other players, and I couldn't be happier to have Lisa at soccer practice today. Two of the best things in my life combined—what more could I wish for?

Out of this cheerful mood, I asked Mitchell, "Up to being captain of the other scrimmage team today?"

"Sure. Want to pick players in turn?" he replied and his gaze skated over to Lisa. When he winked at her, I knew he was going to pick her first.

But I couldn't let this happen, so I laid a possessive arm around her shoulders and told Mitchell, "Yep, you can pick first. But not her."

Lisa stopped abruptly, and since I didn't let go of her, I was dragged to a halt, too. The two of them stared at me like I'd just told them aliens had landed on the school's roof. It didn't bother me. I had plans. Pulling my arm away from Lisa, I made sure to skim my fingers through her soft ponytail. Then I gave her my sweetest *you-have-all-my-attention* smile. "Play with me?"

Tony looked seriously surprised, but the dude knew to shut up now and let her answer.

She seemed a bit uncertain, but finally she drawled, "O—*kay*."

Holy cow, that was it! She'd chosen my team over Tony's. I felt the urge to victory-punch the air.

Tony clapped his hands once, obviously approving. "Cool. Let's play some ball, guys," he exclaimed and ran ahead, starting to pick his players.

We followed him at a slow stroll, and I took the chance to ask, "Do you know how to play soccer, Matthews?"

She shrugged. "Kick the ball into the goal?"

"Yeah, that and a little more." I chuckled. So we were facing a small problem here. I rubbed my neck, feeling a bit lost because there wasn't enough time to lay out all the rules for her. "For now, just don't touch the ball with your hands and try not to kick it past those white lines."

When I pointed out the boundary lines to her, she frowned at me. "You know, I'm not a complete imbecile."

I knew that. But I also knew she'd never played soccer before. To hell with it, today wasn't about winning. It was only about having Lisa on my team. And to my shocked surprise, she played a good game. Her kicks were hard, and she didn't catch the ball with her hands when it came racing her way. She ducked twice to avoid getting hit instead of stopping it, but that was okay.

After the first half, Lisa even did a solo run toward the goal parallel to Susan Miller, who was playing for Tony's team today. The book lover dropped back, and several guys shouted, "Offside!"

Lisa stopped before the goal, her sweet face knitted with

confusion. I headed over and grabbed the ball. "Never mind. I'll explain this tomorrow." Kicking the ball to Ramirez, I cast a glance back over my shoulder and praised her, "Nice shot."

But she hadn't taken that last incident well. Actually, it seemed to have taken all the spirit out of her, and she kept a low profile somewhere at the back of the field. With some kicks toward her, I tried to get her back into the game, but she didn't make it easy for me. And then a collision with Chloe did the rest.

I didn't see exactly if it was an accident or a deliberate foul, but Lisa dropped to the grass, holding her shin, moaning something awful.

"Come on, guys! Play fair!" I shouted, staking Chloe with a hard glare as I jogged over to Lisa. Grabbing her hand, I pulled her up. "You okay?"

She only nodded, but her eyes were glistening with tears. I knew if I tended to her now, she'd just feel all the more embarrassed, so I let it go. But I kept a close eye on her.

It didn't take long for Chloe to foul her again, but this time Lisa let go of a round of cuss words that made the toughest guys on our team turn her way, looking impressed. Including me. It was clear Chloe had gone after Lisa for a reason, so I grabbed the blonde by her arm after the game and told her in no uncertain terms that fouling team members was off the mark and that she'd be off the team if she didn't take my advice to stop. Seriously pissed, Chloe went straight for the parking lot and drove off with screeching tires, which was fine with me. She was a good player, but if she caused a riot in my team, I wouldn't hesitate to kick her out.

I guessed Lisa had left while I was dealing with Chloe and returned to the bench to grab my backpack, but luckily she hadn't. She came walking my way when I turned around, but she also had company. Tony was with her, and I wondered if this was my fault. If Chloe hadn't been off so fast, he might now be leaving the grounds with her and not with Lisa. I gritted my teeth, cast a quick look at her leg that had already taken on a nice shade of blue, and said, "Put ice on that ankle. I want you fit tomorrow."

Jealous to a point where I hated myself, I didn't wait for her to respond, just walked off to my car and drove home. I told myself that they wouldn't be hanging out all evening, that they probably just rode home together. But in my head I couldn't get rid of the image of Mitchell tending to her hurt leg. Touching it, rubbing it, giving her a soft massage. One that I wanted to give her.

I took a long shower, trying to burn those thoughts away with the hot water, but it didn't work. During dinner with my parents, I could hardly concentrate on my meal.

"Is everything okay, son?"

"Hm?" I looked up to find my dad's concerned eyes on me. "Yeah, everything's fine," I said quickly and finished my meal.

Heading back upstairs to my room, I only wanted this evening to be over, so another day with Lisa could begin. And then I saw my phone blinking with a new text coming in. It was from an unknown sender, which was strange considering I had over three hundred contacts saved on my cell. Slumping on the bed, I opened the message.

DON'T NEED TO TRAIN TOMORROW. AND I WANT OFF THE TEAM. LISA (MATTHEWS)

Shit, she had my number and I didn't have hers? This was a first for me. But when the initial joy over her texting me dimmed, I frowned at the words on the screen. She wanted off? *No way!*

I'd already started a reply. DON'T EVEN THINK ABOUT— But then I broke off, studying the blank wall above my desk. Why did she want to leave the team? Maybe I should tell her that I talked to Chloe and she wouldn't have to suffer any more attacks from Tony's new sweetheart. But what if it wasn't that? Her leg had looked really bad. Maybe she was seriously hurt.

I deleted what I'd started to type and wrote instead: DOES IT HURT THAT MUCH? Then I hit send and, like a stupid preschooler, I kept staring at the black screen, waiting and hoping for another text to come in. I even got excited when the display started to blink again.

NO, LEG IS FINE. I'M JUST DONE WITH SOCCER. THANKS FOR YOUR HELP. BYE

What the *hell?* This was bad. And I refused to let her get off just like that. Not by sending a stupid text message. If she wanted out, she'd have to face me first. And suddenly it hit me like a stone on the head. Mitchell. He'd let the bomb go off.

I thumbed through my contacts until I found his number and called.

"Hey," he answered after the third ring.

"What the hell is going on?"

"What do you mean?"

"I got a text from Matthews," I snarled into the phone.

"Oh."

Oh? Was that all? "What have you done?"

"Um...what did she say?"

"She wants off the team, and it's not because of her leg. You broke the news to her, didn't you?"

Mitchell sounded more than just a little depressed when he said, "Yeah. I told her I'm dating Chloe. Guess she didn't take it well."

"Why do you have to guess? Didn't you stay with her to find out?" That was the least someone would expect from her best friend, I thought.

"She left me standing outside. I didn't follow her in. She looked really miserable, and I don't think she'd have liked me there."

"I see." Didn't mean I had to understand. I would have gone after her whether she'd wanted it or not. But for now, that was all I needed to know. And it was probably no use trying to make her change her mind about playing soccer.

Mitchell cleared his throat. "Hey, listen, dude. You two seem to get along really well these days. I mean with the training and all. Would you mind taking care of her a little?"

Fuck, yes! There was no need to ask me. I was all set to give her the strong shoulder she needed to lean on.

But apparently, that wasn't what Mitchell meant. "It would help if you could steer her thoughts into another direction for a while. You're cool with girls, and I think she'd appreciate your charm. Don't get me wrong, you don't have to get personal with her. Just a little flirting, so she doesn't keep thinking about Chloe and me all the time."

"You want me to *distract* her?"

"Yeah, just for a while. Until she gets over it."

How seriously awful was that from someone who claimed to be her best friend? But then I'd intended to be around Lisa, whether he'd asked me to or not. That he approved was just a bonus. "Okay, I'll do it. She's a nice girl, and hanging out with her is fun." I paused for a moment then added, "And I still think she's a way better choice than Chloe. Just don't come back whining when it doesn't work out between the two of you, because by the time you realize it, Lisa might have chosen someone else." *Me.*

"All right."

We hung up, and I sat there in my room for a long moment, wrapping my mind around the shit that was going on. Distract Lisa. What a douche bag. I'd distract her, all right. But I'd do it my way, and only because I intended to get her mind free of Mitchell and ready for me. Could turn out to be an interesting adventure. And now nothing was left to stop me. A slow smile crept to my lips as I keyed in another message for Lisa.

OKAY. TALKED TO MITCHELL. SO THE CAT'S OUT?

No answer came to that text, and after a few minutes I considered calling her. But then I had a way better idea. Yeah, it was just the right thing to get her mind off her misery. I typed a new message. CAN YOU SLIP OUT AFTER DARK?

It didn't take long until one came back this time. I PROBABLY COULD. BUT WHY WOULD I DO THAT?

I smirked at the phone while I punched in: DISTRACTION ;-)

She was quick to reply. REALLY, I'M NOT UP FOR MORE TORTURE.

That wasn't quite encouraging, but neither was it a definite *no*. I pushed off the chair and headed to my wardrobe, skimming through the many dress shirts in there. A white one would be just fine for what I had in mind tonight. I rolled up the sleeves, slipped into tattered blue jeans and light gray tennis shoes, and grabbed the Indians cap from my desk lamp. The ball cap had always brought me luck in the past, and I wouldn't leave it behind tonight.

Loping down the wide, winding stairs, I told my mom, who'd just come out of the dining room, that I was off to see Rachel and Phil and that she didn't need to wait up for me. Then I headed out into the garage and started my Audi.

It was already dark when I reached the avenue where Lisa

lived. There was light in her room, and the window was open again with some depressing music drifting out. I thanked God for the high temperatures in California as I said a bit louder than usual, "Get down here, Matthews!"

The volume of the music lowered, and a couple of seconds later, Lisa appeared in the window, dabbing at her cheeks. Yeah, the crying wasn't over yet. "Why did you come?" She narrowed her bloodshot eyes at me. "Can't you read? I said no."

Her tone didn't quite match her annoyed message. In fact, there was this eighty to twenty percent chance that she was actually happy to see me. "You said no *torturing* you. I'm not going to. Now get into some nice clothes, wash your face, and come out."

"I'm not in the mood—"

Blah, blah. I jumped, grabbing a thick branch of the tree, and hoisted myself onto the shed. That shut her up. And it didn't matter what mood she was in. I'd make sure to get her into the right mood if she only gave me a chance.

"May I come in?" I said through a smirk as I walked across the roof of the shed toward her room and climbed inside without waiting for her invitation.

Obviously trying to catch her breath, Lisa stumbled backward away from the window until she landed on her butt on the bed centered in the room with a headboard attached to one wall. There was a cool desk with a computer and tons of books, and a Hello Kitty poster stuck on the door opposite the window.

I sat down on the windowsill and grabbed the edge. "Nice room," I said, then narrowed my eyes at her and added, "*You* look miserable."

"Gee, thanks for the news update," she snarled back.

Okay, I wasn't really prepared for seeing her down like this, though I should probably have known. This made me a bit uncomfortable, and I wished we weren't in a dimly lit room with the soundtrack from *The Lord of the Rings* playing. Lifting my cap, I raked a nervous hand through my hair. "Listen, I totally suck at this whole *want-to-talk-about-it* crap."

"Then why are you here?" She clearly tried to stake me with her cynicism, but I wouldn't let her have it.

I gave a cool shrug. "Perhaps because I'm good at having fun and taking your mind off certain things," I suggested. "So what do you say? Want to come party a little?"

"I think I'll stay home and listen to some music instead."

At this precise moment, she looked as though another party with me was the last thing she wanted in her life, and I saw my plan evaporating. Brilliant. I needed her to come with me, because I knew she'd like it once she stopped thinking about that douche bag, Mitchell.

"Don't do this to yourself," I begged. "No guy is worth it." And before I knew it, I had walked over to her, took her hands, and pulled her up from the bed. "Come on, *Lisa.*" It felt like the right thing to use her first name, just to get us on a more personal level.

And when this really small smile tugged on her lips for a

millisecond, I knew I'd scored. But she stopped it immediately and made a whiny face instead. "I really don't know—"

"I do," I said firmly, and since she'd given in to my pushing in the past few days, I added, "And now stop arguing." We stared at each other's eyes for the length of a breath. It was hard not to reach up and stroke her rosy cheek and that silky soft hair.

In the end she let out a deep sigh. "Can I shower first?"

"Oh, please do that," I said. She really needed some pepping up before we went where I was planning. I dropped onto her bed, all set for waiting until she was ready to leave. But then my gaze fell on a pile of photo albums.

She noticed they were lying there exactly when I did and grabbed them before I could. "Don't. Touch. Anything."

Aye aye, sir! I lifted my hands, palms up to show my innocence. "Nothing," I solemnly swore. But then I couldn't resist mocking her. "Apart from your diary and maybe your lacy underwear."

A set of lovely dimples appeared on her cheeks, but she tried to look more shocked than infatuated.

When she disappeared from the room, heading for the shower, I really intended to be nice and not touch anything. But after a couple of minutes I got bored and started to look around the room. At the end of her bed, a bit of plaid flannel peeked out from under the comforter, and I leaned forward to pull out whatever it was. It turned out to be the bottoms of her jammies, really cute boy shorts. A gray tank top was there, too, and I had a very intense vision of her wearing that as I pressed her against me for a hot good-night kiss.

Stuffing the things back under the quilt, I stood and walked over to her desk. There must have been a pile with a billion books, but nothing that I would be interested in. There wasn't any Stephen King or Joe Hill. Just loads from someone called Kenyon, and there were pictures of half-naked guys on most of them. Hunky guys. Was that Lisa's preference? I looked down at myself, lifting my shirt, and decided if she went for the muscular build, then I was just her man.

Lowering into her desk chair, I spun around a few times, until I started to get dizzy. I did the same amount of spins in the opposite direction, then I stopped, grabbed the edge of the desk, and pulled myself toward it with the chair. It was a nice place to sit and do homework...if you were a girl. Because she had this really terrible poster of *High School Musical* hanging above her desk.

The drawers to my right called to me, and I thought it would be okay to take a look inside, because Lisa had only been gone for five minutes and she wouldn't be back too soon. There were all kinds of notepads in the first drawer, some pens, and a box of tissues—probably for the moments when her books turned into real tearjerkers.

When I moved to the second drawer, I immediately regretted opening it. Holy cow, there lay her diary. I slammed the drawer shut. But after a half-minute of chewing my lip, I opened it again and took out the little book with a heart drawn around the word diary on the front. There could be a page or two about me in it. I gulped, fighting a hopeless battle against my curiosity. Because, let's face it, it wasn't a question of wrong or right, it was simply a matter of *never leave a guy alone in your room.*

With my heart thumping like that of a silly little girl, I opened the book and skimmed to the last entry.

August 17th. That was yesterday. I cut a glance to the closed door, making sure no sound came from outside. Then I started reading...

ANNA KATMORE

CHAPTER 9

Dear Diary,

I don't know what's happening. One moment I think the entire world is okay, and the next—BAM—I'm totally knocked out of my shoes. I'm a soccer player now. Well, I try to be, but we'll see how good an idea that turns out to be. I did it for Tony, because he's been behaving really strangely since he came back from camp. There's this Barbie clone, who doesn't ever leave his side. I hate her.

Yeah, that was totally Lisa. Grinning at the name she'd picked for Summers, I skimmed over the next paragraph to where she pointed out exactly why Chloe was the wrong girl for Tony, and why she was the right one. I couldn't contradict it at any point, but it was the next passage that I read more carefully, because my name stood out.

But that's not the only thing I'm confused about. There was a party at Ryan Hunter's house. And this time, I was there. The evening went from crazy to confusing to blurred to hot. I think Ryan was flirting with me. And holy cow, batman, that guy smells amazing. I woke up in

his bed. Somehow wrapped around him. He touched my
leg, and I forgot how to breathe.

A fuzzy warm feeling streamed through my body at that information. How very nice. I read faster, needing to find out what else she said about that moment with me.

This is totally weird, because I know I'm in love with
Tony, but when Ryan Hunter smiles, something happens
to me. ~~Something that makes me go stupid and dreamy~~
~~over him.~~ I never thought I'd go for demonic black
instead of angelic blond, but that's just what's happening.
This afternoon, I threw Tony out of my room because I
couldn't stop thinking about Hunter. He has those
beautiful eyes that remind me of—

The door opened. Shit! In a panic-reflex I snapped the diary shut, jumped out of the seat, and hid it behind my back. I held my breath, totally ready to find an excuse for snooping in her personal stuff. But it wasn't Lisa coming in. In the doorway, looking as shocked as I was, stood a much older version of Lisa with her hair cut to her shoulders.

"Hello—" With all the surprise, there was no room for accusation in Mrs. Matthews' voice.

"Hi," I said back, with my heart waiting in line for the next beat.

She slowly walked in, carrying a pile of clean clothes, and

scanned around her. "Where is my daughter?" There was a baffled smile on her face, which made her look a lot friendlier than one would expect from a mother coming into her grounded daughter's room, finding a total stranger inside.

"She's having a shower." I dropped the book into the drawer again and closed it with a small step backward then leaned against the desk.

Only a little taller than Lisa, Mrs. Matthews didn't match my six-foot-two, so when she put the clothes on a chair next to the wardrobe and turned back to me, she tilted her head a little to look at my face. "And you are?"

Totally screwed. I crossed the room to her and reached out one hand, which she immediately took. "My name is Ryan Hunter, ma'am. I'm a friend of Lisa's. We play soccer together."

She didn't let go of my hand. Frowning, she searched my face. "You're Dr. James Hunter's son, right?"

I nodded.

It was cute how a woman in her mid-forties was stunned speechless in her own house. She looked back at the door, stroking her lips with one finger. Then she faced me again. "Just how did you get in here? I know you didn't come through the front door."

I coughed and rubbed the back of my neck. "Um, no. I actually came in through the window."

Suddenly she laughed, and I liked it because she sounded exactly like Lisa. "You guys really make that a habit," she said, reminding me that I wasn't the only one coming in that way.

"Yeah...for what I have planned, this was the only option." I grimaced, but it was too late to find excuses. The truth was probably the best way to deal with this awkward situation.

"And what *have* you planned?"

Taking a deep breath, I squared my shoulders. "I'm going to kidnap your daughter."

"Oh, really?" Mrs. Matthews took a small step back and folded her arms over her chest. "And may I ask why?"

"Because I think she needs a little distraction. She's having a really bad day."

Abandoning her recently adopted defense, she suddenly made a compassionate face. "I noticed something was wrong with her today, but she didn't tell me what happened." Coming forward, she placed a hand on my forearm. "Do you know what it is?"

"Yes, ma'am, I do. But I can't tell you. That's her choice, not mine." Automatically, I put a little distance between us. "But if you want Lisa to feel better as much as I do, then it would help if you could bend the rules tonight and let me steal her."

To my absolute astonishment, she didn't throw me out for that. Instead, she seemed to actually deliberate my words. "You look like a nice boy. And I know Lisa is hurting a lot today. If I let her go with you, will you promise to take care of her?"

The thing about being a nice guy, she probably just said that because she knew my dad. Everyone knew Jim Hunter, the vet. No one believed his son could be any less honorable than

ANNA KATMORE

him. Lucky me.

In a conceding gesture, I lifted my hands and told her, "I promise to bring Lisa back in one piece...and happy."

"I'll take your word for that, young Hunter." She pointed a manicured nail in my face. "And she'd better be back in her room before one o'clock."

"Absolutely." What a cool mom. She reminded me a lot of my own, and I could totally picture getting acquainted with her as the mother of my girlfriend. There was just one more thing. "Would you mind if we didn't tell Lisa that you found me in here?" *Reading her diary...*

"You still want to *kidnap* her?"

"Mm-hm." I nodded and grinned. "It would make the night a little more adventurous for her. And help her forget."

Lisa's mom heaved a deep sigh. "All right. I won't tell if you don't." It was adorable how much crap she put up with just to see her daughter happy again. She walked to the door, but before leaving, she cast me a glance back over her shoulder. "It's because of a boy, right? I'm guessing it's about Tony?"

Pressing my lips together, I gave a helpless shrug.

"I see. You're a *good* friend." She closed the door silently behind her.

I exhaled a deep, relieved breath and dragged my hands down my face. Shit. That was a close call. I'd already envisioned myself being dragged out the front door by my collar.

Giving up the hope of getting a chance to read more of Lisa's diary, I sat back on her bed and worked on my poker face as I waited the remaining minutes until she came back from her shower. Unfortunately, I seemed to overdo it.

Her first expression when she saw me still sitting on her bed was one of total mistrust. "You look too innocent. What have you done?" she growled.

"Nothing. I've been sitting here since you left and it bored the hell out of me," I lied, taking in the low neckline of her purple T-shirt. It stretched nicely over her boobs and flat stomach, ending half an inch above her dark blue jeans. Holy shit, she looked delicious.

"Why don't I believe that?"

Giving an innocent shrug, I rose from the bed and nodded at the open window. "Shall we?"

"I guess I don't have a choice, do I?"

"Nope." I took her hand and pulled her over the windowsill onto the shed. Holding both her wrists in a tight grip, I lowered her as much as I could without falling headfirst off the roof. There was no chance to put her down on the ground, so when her feet dangled about three feet above the ground, I said, "I'm going to let go now. It's not a far fall."

With her eyes on my face, she nodded, not all too happy about my plan.

"On three," I told her. "One, two, three—" I loosened my grip until she slipped away and landed nicely in her garden, bending her knees and touching the ground for balance. When she straightened and looked all right, I swung onto a branch of the nearby tree and made my way down there.

We sneaked out of her garden and walked to my car. I wondered if Mrs. Matthews was spying through the window, and it was then that I remembered what Lisa had told her *dear diary* about me. So I didn't only smell good, I smelled *amazing*. And my smile turned her gaga. I looked down at her with a jumpy feeling in my chest. All this information made me believe she just might be startlingly vulnerable to me.

Out on the pavement, Lisa sneaked a suspicious side glance at me. It prompted me to test my theory, so I tilted my head slightly and smirked a little with just one corner of my mouth tilting up. As if in response, Lisa narrowed her eyes at me briefly, but an instant later, her cheeks took on a rosy color, and her lips curved up. She looked away.

Oh boy, I'd found her trigger. And it was as simple as a smile. If I'd had any idea, I would have done it more often in the past. But then, with her mind set on Mitchell, she might not have even seen it.

I led her to my Audi parked on the other side of the street. A stunned expression settled on Lisa's face as she scanned it from back to front. "Nice car."

"Thanks." The Audi was a babe magnet, so I wasn't surprised she liked it. "You have your license?"

Her gaze lifted to me. "Yeah, got it last summer."

"Want to try her out?" Since I'd been away for most of the summer, the car was still brand new, and I hadn't let anyone drive it. Not even Justin when he begged on his knees. That I offered her the exclusive chance surprised even me. But then, she'd certainly enjoy it, and I really wanted to see her happy again. I'd figured out that I couldn't handle her sad eyes.

"Why?" Lisa demanded with a startled laugh.

I shrugged then opened the door on the driver's side for her and leaned one arm on it. "Fun. And distraction." She looked more than a little skeptical, so I added with a mocking tilt of my brows. "Unless you're chicken."

That swayed her. With a broad show-off grin, she planted her butt behind the steering wheel. "How fast does *she* go?"

I liked how Lisa called my baby a *she* like me. "I promise you'll never find out." Tossing the keys into her lap, I slammed the door shut and walked to the other side. Being the passenger in my own car was a new experience. One that made me a little uncomfortable—not because I didn't trust Lisa's driving skills, but because I preferred to be in control of things. Always.

Lisa fumbled with the seat, adjusting it to her height, then pushed the button and tipped on the gas to coax out a mighty roar from the engine.

"Think you can handle manual?" I asked.

She didn't answer but just flashed a *you-bet* grin at me. Without any trouble, she steered the car out of the lot then started a cozy cruise down the road.

"Is that all you can do?" I mocked her, casting an exaggerated glance at the speedometer. "This car wasn't made for strolling. It's a fucking race car."

From her chewing her lips, I could read that she really wanted to try the Audi, but she seemed a little concerned about whatever—tickets, accidents, hitting something.

"You're thinking too much, Matthews." I sneered when she cut a glance to my side. "Let go and ball the jack."

It didn't take any more convincing. With the engine howling beautifully, I was pressed into the seat. That was fun. And I knew she had some, too, as she raced my baby to the beach.

I had her take a right turn at the ocean. "Have you ever been to Club Tuscany?"

She gave me an appalled look. "I'm sixteen for another few weeks. Of course not."

"Ah, right." Sometimes she behaved a lot older than that. Sometimes a lot younger...I didn't care. I'd take her at any age.

"How old are you?" she wanted to know then.

"Eighteen."

"Since *when*?"

July first. She'd come to watch Tony at practice that day and she hadn't said happy birthday. "Last month."

Her brows furrowed to a line. "But that's still not old enough to go clubbing."

"It is when your brother-in-law owns the club." I had never had any trouble getting in. Paul, the bouncer, knew me, and Rachel would always cover for me if anyone was snooping around, demanding a license. "Follow that road for another ten miles." I gave Lisa directions, then scooted a little lower in the seat and pulled my cap deeper down my face. She handled my car quite well on her own, and there was no need for me to watch like a driving instructor. In fact, it was pretty cool to have a chauffeur for once. It gave me time to study her delicate hand on the gearshift while thinking about her diary confessions. So, she liked it when I touched her. What else did she like about me? I should have pocketed that diary and read every little bit she'd said about me in there. It was too damn tempting to know everything.

A quarter of an hour later, we reached the outskirts of San Luis, and I directed her to the big building with a dark red façade that had "Club Tuscany" spelled in huge, beaming letters across the second-floor level.

Lisa cut the engine and climbed out. When I walked around the car, Paul already had her captured with his most intimidating glare. "You need to wait till you turn twenty-one to get in, sweetness," he said, making her back off immediately.

"Hi, Paul. She's with me," I told him and tucked Lisa under my arm, realizing with a start how very well she fit in there. "Is Rachel in tonight?"

"Hey, Ryan. Didn't know you were coming," Paul answered and pulled down the evil bouncer masquerade, replacing it with a welcoming expression. "Rachel won't be in until later, but Philip's here."

"Cool." We bumped fists, then he opened the door for us, and I dragged a shy Lisa with me.

"Is Rachel your sister?" she whispered.

I used my normal voice when I told her, "Yeah. Philip is her husband. He's cool. You'll like him."

The stomping beat grew louder the farther we walked down the windowless hall dimly lit by neon bars, but Lisa pulled on my arm to stop me. "I don't think I should be here," she whined. "On second thought, you shouldn't be here either."

"You worry too much." I pulled her on, giving her no chance to back out. "I'm here almost every weekend. Everyone knows me. And no one will bother you."

I pushed open the thick metal door in front of us. A cloud of dry smoke and sweat immediately stabbed us in the face. The strobe light made focusing impossible, but I knew my way around here and maneuvered us through the bumping and grinding crowd of clubbers. "C'mon, let's dance."

The word *dance* caused Lisa's pace to shift down a gear, but I'd come here for a few reasons, and feeling her body close to mine was definitely one of them. Holding her hand tight, I dragged her along to the middle of the dance floor, then I turned her around and pressed her against me. Her skin and hair were the only things that smelled good in this place, and I dragged in a deep breath when I lowered my head to hers. "Loosen up, Matthews. You're supposed to be having fun." Giving her a soft push, I twirled her under my arm, then caught her again, and pressed my lips to her ear. "Or at least look like you are."

Lisa laughed, but I could also feel her shivering slightly every time I hugged her tight against my chest. Mmm, it was just the way I wanted her to react to me. Spinning her around, I caught her with her back to my front, running my palm from just underneath her breasts down over her stomach until my hand lay splayed over the small strip of naked skin on her belly. With gentle moves, I made her roll her body with mine to the music.

"What are you doing?" she shouted over her shoulder between hiccups of shy laughter.

Nuzzling her temple, I said in her ear, "Distracting you." I moved her again and loved how her body rubbed against mine, making me go wild for her. "Is it working?"

She gave me no answer to that question and I wanted to bite her earlobe for it. It was probably a good thing Phil came in at that minute and motioned for me to come over as our gazes caught across the room, because otherwise, I just might have dragged Lisa back out to my car to make out for the rest of the night.

Lisa smoothed her T-shirt, which had turned into a mess from my holding her, as we headed over to the oblong bar where Phil served some drinks to a couple of patrons. When they left, he grabbed two cans of Coke from the fridge and placed them in front of Lisa and me. Since there were no speakers above the bar, we could talk in an almost normal volume back here.

"Phil—Lisa," I introduced them. "Lisa, this is Phil, my older sister's husband."

Lisa shook hands with him then guzzled down what seemed to be three quarters of the Coke in one go. I helped her onto one of the high, leather bar stools and took a casual stance between her legs, turned to face the bar.

Phil knew I had no girlfriend, so he asked, "You know each other from school?"

"Sort of. We play soccer together now," I told him. "New co-ed team."

"Really? That's cool." He turned an interested face to Lisa and pulled his shoulder-length hair into a ponytail. "Do you like it?"

"Yeah, it's great. Love the training."

What did she just say? I turned toward her, raising one brow.

"What?" she mouthed.

I tucked her soft strands behind her ear and leaned closer. "I still have the text where you say you're done with soccer, *Lisa.*"

I noticed how she swallowed at my taunt. But then she leaned back just a little and looked me sternly in the eye. "Did you really not know my name before I sent you that message?"

Ah, girl, if only you knew. But I wouldn't tell her. Not now, anyway. With a laugh, I shrugged it off. "Why, Matthews? You were devoted to Mitchell. What would I care?"

That earned me a hard shove against my shoulder, but she grinned, anyway. "You're such an ass, you know."

"I've been told girls go for that." I winked at her then drank from my Coke, my eyes still on her face. I enjoyed how her cheeks flushed a delicious pink. She tried to hide behind her can as she took another sip, but her gaze returned to me, and the moment we shared looking at each other filled me with a desire for her that topped everything I'd known in the past.

I was abruptly pulled out of that moment when a girl looped her arm around my neck and pressed a kiss to my cheek. For the length of a heartbeat I froze, scared this was one of my acquaintances coming over to say hello at the utterly wrong moment. Then I looked into familiar brown eyes.

"Hi, little brother," Rachel said and shoved her long black hair back over her shoulder.

"Hey, Rach," I said back and relaxed. I knew she was burning to hear who the girl by my side was, so I waited until she came around, then I told her, "This is the friend of a friend. Her name is Matthews, and she's on my soccer team. Well was...is...I don't know."

The girls shook hands, and after a short scowl at me, Lisa said, "My name is Lisa."

"Don't mind him. The oaf was never comfortable with first names," Rach sold me out. "I'm lucky—I'm his sister."

Yeah, right. "That doesn't mean a thing, *Carter.*" I pulled her hair like I used to do as a child when I wanted to annoy her and laughed. Then I popped open another soda and clinked cans with my brother-in-law.

"So, the friend of a friend, huh?" I heard Rachel say to Lisa, and she sounded way too curious. "Where is that friend?"

"Not here," I told her with an evil grin, letting her know that for tonight, Lisa was *my* friend. Lisa seemed to enjoy that fact just the same as she met my gaze.

ANNA KATMORE

The only one who didn't look happy was Rachel. "Just when will you grow up and settle for *one*?"

Luckily, Phil backed me up as he leaned over the bar and kissed my sister. "He's young, baby. He has time."

"I know." Rachel gave me a wry look. "I'm just waiting for the day that a girl sees through you...and decides to like you anyway."

"Yep, me, too." I really was. And hopefully, Lisa would be just the one.

"That calls for a drink!" Philip announced all of a sudden, and I could have murdered him for that.

But instead, I froze, and a weird shower skittered down the back of my neck. What the hell—he couldn't be serious. This wasn't me bringing a random girl to the club to have some meaningless fun. It was *Lisa*. And I would do many things with her right now, but I wouldn't ruin our first kiss with the stupid game Phil had in mind.

CHAPTER 10

PHIL PLACED TWO small glasses on the counter and shoved one toward me. Immediately, I passed it on to my sister, not intending to play along. "You can have your drink with Rach. I'll skip tonight."

"This game is stupid," Rach pointed out with a disgusted grunt.

But Philip ignored her and made a wry face at me. "You pass? With that beautiful drinking partner?"

She was beautiful, but that was not the point. "I'm not having this drink with *her.*"

"Why? Is she shy?"

Maybe she was, but who cared? Above all, Lisa was special. And Phil needed to understand that. "She's too nice," I said, determined to put an end to this. At the same time, I noticed Lisa's attention focused on me, and it was anything but pleasant.

"Ah, she's a prude then," Phil concluded wrongly.

That seriously pissed Lisa off. "I'm not a prude! And I'm standing right beside you, so I would appreciate it if you told me what the hell you two are talking about."

Trying to soothe and reassure her, I stroked her cheek

158   ANNA KATMORE

with my knuckles. "She's decent," I corrected Phil.

"Yeah, and decent is a shit word for prude," Lisa muttered, dropping her gaze, but then she looked back at me and scowled again. Or maybe it wasn't a scowl after all? "So, why don't you want to do with me whatever you're used to doing with other girls when you come here?"

Oh, girl, if only you knew how very much I want to do just that with you. With everything I'd found out from yesterday's diary entry, I could just imagine how the thought of my denying her would hurt her. It made her vulnerable to me, and in that exact moment, I realized with a start how much this appealed to me. I always thought I'd go for the sassy and strong type of girl, which Lisa definitely could be if she wanted to. But it was her vulnerable side that attracted me the most.

And yet, I couldn't take advantage of it. Everybody's first kiss should be romantic. Something Lisa would remember for the rest of her life. She'd hate me if I spoiled this for her. But heck, when I looked at her cute pout, I could hardly withstand the temptation. "You don't know what you're asking for, Matthews," I growled.

"Well, it won't kill me to find out, right?"

It wouldn't kill her, no. But *she* might kill me, if I screwed this up. Her eyes fastened on mine. Holy shit, what if I just gave it a try? If I made it good for her, she might acquire a taste for it. For *me*.

Taking a deep breath, I drawled, "Okay. But remember, I gave you fair warning."

Lisa looked like she couldn't make up her mind between being stubborn or scared as hell of what I was going to do with her in a minute. Well, she didn't have to be scared. The girls I'd been out with bragged about me being a good kisser for a reason.

With a quick glance at Philip, I nodded, and he filled the two glasses with tequila, obviously happy about the new development. Rachel grabbed the bottle from his hand when my glass was only half-full. "That's enough for him," she insisted.

That was okay. There could have been water in the shot and I wouldn't have minded, because the most essential part of this game was actually not the drink but the half slice of lime that Phil had just placed on my glass.

While my anticipation grew to a point that reached my pants, Lisa looked every bit ready to back out. I gave her a half-smile, one which I knew made her go *stupid and dreamy*. "You still game?"

"I don't have to drink this, do I?" she whispered uncertain.

"No, you don't," I assured her, hoping she'd keep up her bravery. "That's for me. You only assist with the lime."

She looked at the juicy fruit then back at me and nodded. "Game on."

That was my cue. Smiling to myself, I took the lime off the tequila, clinked my glass to Philip's, and held the slice out to Lisa. "Bite."

"What?"

"*Bite*," I said again as I put the glass down and dragged

the brim of my cap around to the back of my head so it wouldn't poke her in the eye. Then I knocked back the shot, the sharp taste of liquor burning down my throat.

Lisa's eyes staked mine as she leaned forward and bit into the fruit I held out to her. With a grimace, she jerked away. All right, that would do. Tossing the slice into my empty glass, I reached around her neck and slipped my hand under her soft hair. There was no time to think, or I might change my mind...for her sake, not for mine.

Her eyes grew wide with surprise as I yanked her toward me, and with my mouth pressed gently against hers, I slid my tongue across her tender bottom lip, licking away the sour taste of lime juice. Just because she deserved it for her earlier sweet pout, I gave her lip a gentle nip. Then I went for the full taste. With a little more pressure in the right place, I worked her mouth open with mine.

I realized that I had stunned her breathless, but when I roamed her mouth with my tongue, she was ready to give back in full. In a sensually slow motion, I stroked her tongue with mine, savoring the beguiling mix of Coke and lime together with Lisa's sweetness.

God, how long had I been waiting for this moment? For this first real taste of her. It seemed like forever, and it was totally worth the wait. Getting high from her amazing smell and from how soft her skin felt against my palm when I caressed her neck and cheek, I didn't want to ever stop kissing her. But if I also wanted her to live through this, I knew I had to pull away, so she would finally start breathing again.

I pulled a tiny inch back and told her with a soft, low, and utterly happy voice, "Thanks for your help with the lime."

"Uh-huh." Her gorgeous eyes turned a darker shade of green with innocent passion. "Anytime."

I loved her being baffled, because her luscious lips were slightly parted, inviting me back in. She stared at me as though we were the only people in the room. Hell, if that were true, she'd be lying on that bar now, trapped underneath me, and a simple kiss wouldn't fucking do.

Rachel squeezed in between me and Lisa, sending a disapproving scowl at Phil and me. "Look what you did, you oafs. You scared the poor girl."

"Nah, she isn't scared." Giving up my place next to Lisa, I winked at her over my sister's shoulder. "I bet she enjoyed it."

And now the sweetest smile slipped to Lisa's face. With a light blush, she turned her head away.

Oh yes, vulnerable. And so up for more. I was dying to know what she'd be writing about in her diary tonight.

While Rachel fired a volley of questions at Lisa that showed she'd noticed my genuine interest in her, I turned to Phil and had another soda with him. We ranted about the three guys on stage that were performing a song by OneRepublic.

"When was the last time you stood up there and sang karaoke?" Phil asked with an obvious hint.

It had been months. And the last time wasn't such a great success, because Justin and I had sung a duet after we'd drunk a little too much. But it was always fun to stand on stage and have the crowd cheering for us. "It's been a while. You know it's hard to find a partner who can actually sing."

Philip gave a subtle nod toward the girls.

"Rachel?" I asked, narrowing my eyes.

Phil shook his head, moving his eyes toward Lisa and back at me.

Now I quirked my brows and said a bit lower, "Lisa?" Sliding a look over to her, I considered the idea. She didn't look to me like someone who'd like to become the center of attention in a stuffed club. "She'd never agree."

"She would have never agreed to the lime kiss either. But she obviously liked it a lot."

I laughed out loud. "You think I should surprise her?"

"What's the worst that can happen?"

"She hates me afterwards and doesn't ever talk to me again?"

Phil chuckled. "Good point."

I listened to the next song, deciding that the guys earlier were a lot better than the two girls who were blaring a Whitney Houston song now. Lisa and I could do better than that.

When I overheard how my sister was starting to compare Lisa's and my preferences in food, I made up my mind quickly and figured it was time to cut the conversation off and save Lisa from the grilling.

"She's the devil in disguise, hunting for potential in-laws," I warned Lisa. "Don't let her make you sign anything."

Rachel slapped me on the shoulder for that remark, but I didn't care and just grinned at her, because we both knew I was right. Then I took Lisa's hand and pulled her off the bar stool. "Let me save you from the Spanish Inquisition," I said in her ear and made her follow me through the crowd.

A few feet away from the stage, she probably realized what I had in mind, and she pulled me to a stop. "You're kidding me, right?"

"Nope." I added a smile to that. Something she could concentrate on and forget the panic that now caused her hand to shake in mine. And indeed, she walked with me up the stairs onto the stage, though a little reluctant.

I left her by the microphone for a second to tell the DJ which song he should play. When I turned around again, Lisa made a break for the stairs. With my arm around her waist, I stopped her and dragged her back to the mike.

"You're so going to pay for this," she hissed, but I thought she was more thrilled at the thought of singing than frightened. Otherwise, I wouldn't have made her come up with me.

Leaning down to her ear, I told her, "You can hate me later. Now, we sing."

When the music rolled out, Lisa stared at me with huge eyes. I figured it was up to me alone to perform the first lines of *Country Roads*. I hugged her tight against me and adjusted the mike to my height, then I sang, and Lisa was silent.

The emotions playing out in her face screamed: *I'm going to kill you for this!* And I thought, okay, if I was going to die anyway, we could at least have some fun first. It was her turn to sing, and I held the microphone in front of her kissable mouth.

Her nails dug into my stomach where she clamped my shirt, and I could feel her heart hammering in her chest where she pressed against me. "Sing," I mouthed and gave her the most encouraging look manageable.

Lisa grimaced and squeezed her eyes shut. But she opened her mouth and within a few seconds her panicky croak turned into a really beautiful singing voice. Her eyes opened again, and she looked at me with wonder, like she was totally amazed at herself and how well she was doing. Soon her clawed fingers uncurled, and she pressed her palm against my chest. I placed my hand on top of hers, trying to give her the safe feeling she needed.

When the crowd started singing with us, her face lit up even more. I got the feeling she was really enjoying herself and figured we could do a little more than just standing poker-stiff. Slipping behind her, I took her hands and lifted them over her head. Together we clapped to the beat, and our audience mirrored us. I stood very close to her, enjoying the nearness, and sang in her ear while she had the mike all to herself. She delivered an amazing show. That was my girl. Vulnerable like a kitten, but strong and brave when she needed to be.

The song's end was drowned out by the clubbers' whistles and shouts, encouraging us to perform another song. I was totally up to it, but this time I thought it better to ask Lisa first. "What do you think?"

"I think I'm going to kill you."

Yeah, I knew that and laughed.

"No way are we doing this again." She grabbed my hand like I'd done with her before and made me follow her down from the stage.

I shrugged and grinned at the expectant crowd as I was dragged away.

When we reached the bar again, Rachel had switched sides and stood with Phil behind the counter now. "That was awesome!" She beamed at Lisa and me together. "You'd really make a sweet couple."

Lisa laughed about that. "Yeah, right."

Yeah, right? Did that mean no? I gave her a wry look and she cast me the same look back, then she stuck her tongue out at me and laughed again.

Okay, Hunter, make something of that, I thought.

A little later, she asked me if it was okay to leave. It was almost midnight, and I remembered that I'd promised to take Cinderella back before one. I let Rachel kiss my cheek as we told them goodbye, and she whispered into my ear that she'd come home tomorrow and intended to get all the details about me and Lisa.

"All right," I surrendered. "But only if you bring cherry cake." She made the best cake in all California, I swear.

Out in the cool air, I took a few deep breaths, getting rid of the dry smoke in my lungs, then I turned to Lisa who pressed her palms to her red cheeks. "Want to drive again?"

She shook her head. "The way I feel right now I might very well wrap your car around a tree."

Still shaky from the excitement, eh? I put my arm around her shoulders like we were already a real couple. She didn't back away. And when her shy hand moved up to rest on my hip, my stomach did a double roll of joy.

Opening the passenger door for her, I let her get in first, then I walked around and made myself comfortable in the driver's seat, readjusting it to my longer legs.

Since Lisa was looking out the side window, I figured she wasn't up for talking, so I switched the radio on but kept the volume low. I liked how her beautiful scent filled the interior and my head. It was hard to concentrate on driving when my thoughts drifted to my right time and again and I remembered how her tender lips had felt beneath mine.

After a few minutes, she turned and studied me instead of the passing streetlamps.

I cut a quick glance toward her. "Did you enjoy yourself tonight?" It was nice to speak in a softer tone again after shouting so much inside the club.

Lisa hesitated a couple of seconds before she answered, "It was okay." Then after a short pause she added, "Actually, it was quite nice."

As I cut another glance at her, she made a point at playfully narrowing her eyes at me. "But I still hate you!"

That coaxed a chuckle from me. "I know." And I didn't mind as long as she stayed in this car with me. "I'm sorry I dragged you into hell on that stage."

"And you *should* be."

A car passed us, and the headlights made me squint for a moment. But when the car had disappeared from the review mirror, I moved most of my attention away from the silent road and back to Lisa. "What about the lime surprise?"

"What about it?"

"Should I be sorry about that, too?"

Lisa let me wait on her answer long enough that my stomach got all butterfly-fluttery. I was holding my breath. Then she said in a nonchalant tone, "Nah. I just should have heeded your warning."

"Yeah. Or maybe...just not." Because as far as I was concerned, it had been one helluva hot kiss, and I wouldn't want to have missed it.

With a lower voice than before, Lisa drawled, "Or maybe not..."

Heck, had she just agreed? "You liked it?" The blush on her cheeks made me smile. "Yeah, you did."

Lisa didn't say anything more about it, but after one last shy look at me, she tilted her head the other way and continued gazing out the window. In the reflection of the glass, I glimpsed her pleased face.

We arrived at her house way too soon.

"Can you park a bit farther up this road?" Lisa asked me then. "I don't want my parents to find out I was gone."

Sunshine, they already know. But I did as she said, and as we got out of the car, I shut my door quickly to keep as much of her nice scent as possible saved inside for the ride home.

I walked her back into her garden at a casual stroll. I liked watching her as we went. Everything about her was perfect. The only thing wrong was that she wasn't tucked under my arm right now. It was definitely worth a try, but Lisa turned her head to my side at that moment, and when her lips curved up, I knew I was caught staring. For a change, this made me feel awkward. Exposed somehow. With a sheepish grin, I rubbed my neck, looking away.

In front of the little shed in her garden, I took a stance with my back to the door and waited for her to put her foot into my laced hands to help her up. She grabbed my shoulders and stepped in, but before I lifted her, I took a second to look into her eyes. "What do you say, Matthews? Shall we do this again sometime?"

Lisa glanced up to her room and back at me. "Maybe we should. But let's wait until my detention is over. I really hate sneaking in and out like a criminal."

I could live with that.

With a strong push, I hoisted her onto the roof and waited until she'd made it to her feet. Sneaking back into her room, she whispered, "Good night."

"Later 'gator," I said back.

Heading back to my car, I could have slapped myself for missing the opportunity to steal a good-night kiss before I'd shot her up onto that roof. By now I was pretty confident she wouldn't have slapped me for it. Heck, what if she'd even expected it and I'd just screwed that chance?

I climbed into the car and banged my head on the steering wheel. I was such an idiot. Maybe I should have sent her a good-night text at least. Just to tell her that I really loved spending the evening with her. And maybe make plans to see her again tomorrow?

Shifting in the seat, I fished in my pocket for my phone and stared at the screen. But then I had a better idea. Way better...

CHAPTER 11

THE WARM NIGHT coated my neck with a layer of sweat as I jogged back to Lisa's house. Underneath her window, I lifted my Indians cap, raked a hand through my hair, and put the cap on again. This was my chance at Lisa, and I wasn't going to ruin it. Not after waiting half my high school years for it.

The light in her room was already off. I could call her to the window now then talk her outside again like a gentleman. Or...I could behave like a guy my age. Turning around, I took a short run toward the tree, jumped, and hoisted myself onto the thickest branch. From there it was only a large step onto the shed's roof. I didn't hesitate a second but strode directly to Lisa's room and ducked through the window.

At that moment, the light went on, and a sharp voice said, "Hunter. What are *you* doing here?"

I looked up and found Lisa standing barefoot in those amazing, hot boy shorts, just a couple of feet away from me. "I forgot something."

She quirked her brows like she questioned my sanity. "You can't just come up here. I'm already in my jammies."

Hell yeah, that was one of the reasons why it had to be *now* and not any other time. "I've never seen anything sexier than those shorts on you." Seizing every inch of her skin with my gaze, I prowled toward her. The longer I looked at her legs, the more goose bumps she got.

Lisa took a step back for each I took toward her. She wouldn't escape. Finally, she was stopped by her bed, and I still had one foot of distance to overcome. But I stopped when she did, and hooked my finger into the waistband of her mouthwatering shorts instead. Pulling her toward me, I locked gazes with her. Lisa's eyes were wide and shiny. Her mouth hung slightly open as she moved her hands up and placed them flat on my chest. My pecs twitched in response to this intimate touch, and I was ready to rip my shirt open, so I could feel her warm hands on my skin.

Lisa's breathing hitched noticeably. "You forgot something?" It was a shy croak. "What?"

Seriously, we had talked enough tonight. Now was the time for satisfying a deeper need within me. I pulled my Indians cap off and tossed it onto the bed, never breaking eye contact with her. With one arm around her delicate waist, I pulled her into me and thrust my other hand into her silky hair.

Lisa's breath came fast against my skin. My gaze dropped from her eyes to her lush lips. I knew I was going to die if I couldn't sample them again this minute. Slowly, I leaned down and rendered her mine.

Pressing a feather-light kiss to her lips, I waited to see if she would keep breathing this time. Oh yes, she did. And more. Her soft little hands moved up and around my neck, her fingers threading through my hair. It made me go crazy and wild. Growling, I pulled her tighter against me and invaded her sweet mouth with my tongue. The Coke and lime taste was gone, replaced by the taste of minty toothpaste.

In slow strokes, I started playing with her tongue. Lisa shivered in my arms. She rose on her toes to match my height just a little more, pressing herself in a dangerously seductive way against me. If there really could be butterflies in one's stomach, there was definitively one playing havoc in mine now.

She didn't like it when I broke the kiss, but I inched back anyway then leaned my brow against hers, getting a grip on myself. Being back in her room, I'd remembered her diary and realized I could make up for reading it by giving her a little truth about myself. Something she might like to know.

"By the way," I said softly. "I've known your name since the very day you first came to watch Mitchell's soccer practice in ninth grade, *Lisa*."

A smile tugged hard on the corners of her lips, but apparently she didn't want to let it come. Instead she teased, "Have you, really?"

If she wasn't going to smile, then I wasn't either, so I pressed my lips together, but I knew it wouldn't work. I nudged her nose with the tip of mine. "Mm-hm."

The next instant, I found my lips on hers once more. A low moan escaped her, which I cupped with my mouth, and it took me to the edge of self-control. To hell with *gentle*. Raking back her hair, I tilted her face farther up and ravished her mouth with a deep, ferocious kiss.

She stood only at the beginning of learning, but she was quick and took up with the lust I breathed. In sensual moves, her tongue brushed against mine. She suckled and nipped my bottom lip, groaning when I did the same to hers. Gone wild with longing, I stroked down her neck and spine, finding an easy way underneath her tank top, and explored every little bit of her.

All the shyness abandoned, Lisa utterly melted into my embrace. I placed my hands on her bottom, ready to lift her up so she would wrap her naked legs around my hips. But a hard pull at my collar made me stumble backward, and Lisa slipped away from me.

It was the shock in her eyes that made me realize who had come even before I heard the sharp bellow behind me.

"What the fucking hell— Take your bloody hands off her!"

I was hurled around, and a hard punch to my face broke the skin on my lip.

"No! Tony!" I heard Lisa's strangled shriek as I staggered back. But I caught myself quickly and stopped her with a scowl from rushing to my aid. Sliding my tongue over my bottom lip, I tasted blood. Fucking brilliant. I was going to kill Mitchell for that.

In an instant, I had him trapped between me and the wall, pressing my forearm against his throat. There was a lot of anger in his eyes, covering a layer of hurt. Now I knew why he'd come.

Reconsidering my killer instinct, I eased the pressure on his throat but didn't take my arm away. "I'll let you off this one time because you're my *friend*, Mitchell," I growled. "But do that again and you won't live through the night."

"You don't scare me, Hunter," he snarled back, and the next thing I knew my nose was broken. He must have head-butted me.

That was the end of my patience. Mitchell was dog food. With murder on my mind, I started toward him, but Lisa was suddenly there, squeezed in between us, and her trembling hand pushed against my chest.

"No," she told me, then she turned to Tony and said more fiercely, "*No!* You're not going to do this. Not in my room. And not over me."

There was enough hatred in the room to wipe out Grover Beach, but clearly neither of us wanted to hurt Lisa. She sent me a pleading glance, probably expecting me to be the smarter one and end this. I didn't know how. With her standing between us, we let a minute pass, both bristling with anger. But when she didn't get out of the way, we finally toned it down a notch.

The frightened look in her eyes eased. Now frustration seemed to take over, and she turned away from me, facing Tony. "Why did you come here?"

"I had to make sure this asshole keeps his hands off your body."

He'd fucked up everything from the start and called me the asshole? "You've chosen one helluva moment to show up," I growled cynically over Lisa's shoulder.

"Seems like I'm just in time. You're not going to touch her again."

"I'm sure Lisa can speak for herself and doesn't need *you* to babysit her." Anyway, it was time to get this over with. I wasn't going to hang out here with Mitchell and discuss the matter over Lisa's head. Placing my hands on her hips, I moved her gently to my side. I'd never hurt this girl, but in the condition Tony was in, I couldn't judge his next move, and I just wanted her out of the way. Fixing him with a death glare, I added, "This is none of your business."

"She's my friend and sure as hell *is* my business," Tony spat.

"What's your problem, man?"

"You are. This shit ends now. I didn't ask you to go that far with her."

The hair on the back of my neck lifted and I froze. "Shut. The hell. Up, Mitchell."

But the bastard pointed a finger at me and kept sputtering. "I didn't mean for you to sleep with her when I asked you to distract her."

Shit.

I clenched my jaw, waiting for Lisa to pick up on that. And she sure as hell did. Slowly tilting her head to me, her brows furrowed to a line. "Distract?"

What could I say to make her understand that? "It's not like that—"

"No?" Her voice was a far cry from stable, and tears sprang to her eyes.

I wanted to take her face between my hands, make her look into my eyes and see the truth in there. That for me, it had always been her.

"Bullshit, of course it's like that," Tony snapped before I could even lift my hands to her face. "He called me this afternoon, wanting to know why you'd quit soccer all of a sudden. I asked him to get your mind off—" He broke off, then continued with less wrath in his voice, "Off *us*. I knew you didn't want to see me, but I couldn't stand the thought of you being in your room all alone, crying." He moved a killer scowl to me. "But now that I think of it, it was a crappy idea from the beginning. You deserve better than him. All he wants is to get in your pants. Don't you, Hunter?"

"You don't know anything, you fool!" Did he know me even one bit after all the years we'd been friends?

But at the same time I growled at Mitchell, Lisa asked him, "I deserve better?" She angled her head. "Then who, Tony? *You*?" Everyone caught her cynicism.

Tony came toward her and replied, "I was good enough for you for the past ten years." He was clearly hurting at her words.

But I didn't care. If anything, it made me madder than ever. With a hard shove against his chest, I sent him back against the wall. "*Now* you start to fight for her? You goddamned idiot!"

"I don't have to fight for her. Not with you. She never wanted you."

"She might, now. And that scares the shit out of you, doesn't it?" I knew this was what sent him back to her room tonight. "Giving her up, but not wanting her to be with someone else. You're pathetic."

Lisa walked up beside me and gazed for a long moment at Tony's face. "What's going on? You told me you're dating Chloe. So why are you in my room in the middle of the night?"

Tony didn't answer her, and suddenly everything made sense. "Not hard to guess," I said with a dry, painful laugh. "You slept with Chloe. And she dumped you like I told you she would, didn't she?"

The truth shone in his glistening eyes—visible even for Lisa this time. She backed away, dropping on her bed. Tony went after her, knocking hard against my shoulder, but when he reached for her, she crawled away from him and hissed, "Don't you dare touch me!"

Tony planted one knee on the mattress. "Please, Liz—"

"No!" She slapped him hard on the face. "Just go!" And when he didn't move, she added with a voice gone toxic, "*Now!*"

It would have been enough to make me back away. And Tony did, too. His face scrunched with lines of aching, he pushed past me and climbed out the window.

I waited until he disappeared in the dark garden. Then I slowly turned around to Lisa. A stream of blood ran from my nose down to my lips. Wiping it away with the back of my hand, I told her, "I really didn't—"

"Stop it!" Lisa raised both her palms rendering me silent. "I don't know which of you two disgusts me more tonight. Leave me alone. I'm done with you."

She couldn't mean it. All the crap Tony had told her tonight—she must realize that it was nothing but a blasted lie. "I didn't come because Mitchell asked me to. I came because *I* wanted to see you again."

"Yeah, right. As if I would believe that. Distraction, huh? Tell me, did I look so miserable that you thought my life depended on your mercy?" There was a tiny tear glistening on her cheek as it fell. "Or did you really just want to get in my pants?"

Facing her accusations was something I could deal with. But seeing her cry was something entirely different. It was too much, and I didn't know how to handle it. Not when I was the one who'd made her cry. I pinched the spot between my eyes. "Cut the crap, Lisa. You know that's not true."

"Leave!" She wiped the single tear away, and when she spoke next, her voice was steady. And stone cold. "I don't ever want to see you again."

No. *Please, no*! I couldn't leave her now. There had to be a way to get things straight between us again—to convince her that I never intended to just *play* with her. But that my heart was in this game from the very first moment.

Her gaze only hardened, making it clear there was no chance for us. Not anymore.

My heart ached, and so did the rest of my body when I walked toward her. Leaning down to brace myself on the bed on either side of her, I searched her face one last time for a flicker of hope. There was none.

All right. I had lost what I never really had. And that little bit of hope she'd awoken in me these past few days made the pain unbearable. "For a minute there, I thought I stood a chance. But I guess in the end, Mitchell will still be the lucky one."

Closing that last inch of distance between our faces, I inhaled her pure, beautiful scent one last time. She didn't back away from me, but her eyes said she wouldn't tolerate the tiniest touch right now.

I grabbed my cap from behind her and straightened, pulling the brim deep down my face. "See you around, Matthews."

Pivoting, I strode toward the open window, climbed out, and jumped from the shed. There was no one holding me there. No one telling me to come again tomorrow, so we could talk. No one to say good night. There was only a hurting girl who closed the window behind me.

CHAPTER 12

I HAD NO idea where I was going, but I knew going home wasn't an option for me right now. Racing the car along the highway, I tried to blast my mind free with the music turned up to a deafening level. I was out of town before I knew it, heading south.

No one I knew lived in that area, so at some point I just brought the car to a halt in an empty parking lot and climbed out. The headlights sliced through the pitch-black night, falling on calm waves rolling toward the shore. Sand gnashed underneath my shoes as I walked down the stone steps and crossed the beach toward the sea. Shortly before the sand got wet, I sat down, hugged my legs to my chest, and rested my chin on my knees. I stared out at the ocean, trying to make sense of something I couldn't understand.

Why was it always the things you wanted most that you couldn't have?

No one was there to give me an answer.

After some minutes, the Audi's control system cut the lights and left me brooding in the dark. I didn't move...for hours. Until the sun crept up behind me and slowly warmed my cold and stiff body. My phone went off in my pocket. I had this hurtful hope that Lisa wanted to talk to me. But it wasn't her. The display flashed *Mom.* She'd probably realized my car wasn't around the house and got worried. I didn't answer the call, but I got to my feet and dragged my hurting self to the car. Half falling asleep, I drove home.

Before getting out of my car, I cleaned my face from all the blood, because I didn't want to scare anyone. But the split lip and swollen nose would give me away, no matter what. As I slipped in through the front door, the big grandfather clock in the living room chimed nine o'clock. I was careful not to make a sound when I shut the door, but my mom had certainly heard my car coming home. There was no escaping her worried inquisition.

"Ryan, darling, where have you been?"

I knew it was bad when she called me *darling.* It always indicated she'd been worried sick about me. She cupped my cheeks and made me look down at her face. "Good gracious! What happened? Did you have an accident?" Then she sucked in a sharp breath. "Or did you get in a fight?"

Taking her hands in mine, I pulled them gently away from my face. "Nothing happened, Mom. I'm all right." As all right as one could be with his heart ripped from his chest and trampled on. "No car crash, no fight." Not a real one anyway. "I'm not hurt, just tired."

"But something must have—"

"Please, Mom. I don't want to talk right now." I must have sounded whiny and aching. Pathetic.

For a stunned mother-son moment, she gazed at my pleading, misty eyes, and it seemed to be enough for her to understand. Everything. "All right, darling. You go up and get into bed. I'll bring you a cup of hot chocolate."

I drank coffee in the morning, and she knew it. But I wouldn't be surprised if there was going to be a marshmallow in the hot chocolate, too. Dragging myself up the stairs was more exhausting than driving the eighty miles home with only one eye open. I kicked my shoes into the corner and stripped down to my boxers on the way into the bathroom. In front of the shower, that last bit dropped too, and I stepped into the stall with a hot spray of water raining down on me. Bracing my palms on the tiled wall, I hung my head, breathing hard into the gush of water. This was the only time that I'd let go of the tears that had choked me the whole night, because the evidence of them would be washed away in the shower.

Half an hour passed, and the rain never stopped. I didn't want to get out of the shower. I'd stay here for as long as my heart was aching like it was clamped in a bear trap. My hands fisted against the tiles, and I pressed my forehead on them. How could my life ever be normal again?

By the time I finally turned off the water, I feared I'd fall asleep standing up. Feebly, I toweled myself dry then wrapped that towel around my hips and shuffled back to my room where I pulled on shorts and a tee. On my nightstand, I found the promised cup of hot chocolate, which had turned cold by now. I didn't care, because I had no intention of drinking it anyway.

Hot chocolate might help if you were sick or sad because your favorite hamster died. But I didn't see what it could do to mend a broken heart. Dumping headfirst into my pillow, I left the rest of the world behind me and hoped to just drift off to oblivious dreams.

I did. But when I woke up again, I realized I'd hardly been knocked out long enough for my hair to dry after the shower. Rolling onto my back, I started to stare at the ceiling...and stopped two hours later when there was a quiet knock on my door.

My mom slipped her head in silently enough not to wake me if I was asleep. When she saw me wide awake, she said softly, "Your dad and I are going to eat lunch in a minute. Don't you want to come down?"

"I'm not hungry," I told her, hoping she would get the hint and leave me alone.

But she came in anyway and sat down beside me, then stroked a gentle hand through my hair. "What happened, darling? Was it about a girl?"

Closing my eyes, I let her caress me, struggling not to grimace for her sake. "Seriously, Mom, I don't want to talk about it." My throat ached when I spoke, and I pressed my lips together to stop them from trembling. Maybe one day I would tell her about last night. But not now, when I could hardly keep myself together.

Jezebel Hunter gave me one of her understanding nods. "I'm here when you need me." Then she left my room on silent feet.

Moving my gaze back to the ceiling, I tried to figure out what I'd done to screw it up with Lisa. I'd been careful, I'd been considerate, I'd been waiting for ages. But maybe that was the whole mistake? Maybe she'd have realized how much she really meant to me if I'd been upfront with her from the start. She wouldn't think I'd been playing a stupid game with her now. And she wouldn't have cast me out of her life.

I don't ever want to see you again.

I wiped my nose with the back of my hand, fighting to blink away a sudden gush of water in my eyes.

In the late afternoon, there was another knock on my door, but this time it was Rachel marching in like she owned the room. She carried a plate on which sat a fat piece of cherry vanilla cream cake. Smiling, she slumped on the mattress and waved the plate in front of my nose. "I brought the cake, you spill."

She couldn't have made it past my mother without gleaning the information that I was in a somewhat *down* mood today. Mom must have encouraged her to come up and find out what had happened.

"Rachel, go away. I don't want to talk to you, or Mom, or anybody else today."

"So it's true." Her face scrunched up. "You're love sick? Could only be that if you're refusing cherry cake. And by the way, you look like shit. Who messed with your face?"

I clenched my teeth behind tight lips. "Doesn't matter.

And now that you've figured me out, Sherlock Holmes, I'd be happy if you could leave me alone."

"No, you wouldn't be happy. You'd just hang out in here all day and drown in self-pity." She scooted farther up on the mattress and placed the cake on my nightstand. "What the heck happened after you and Lisa left last night? You looked totally into each other."

And I totally thought we were. I heaved a sigh, wanting nothing but a little time alone. Was that really asking too much in a house twice as big as my high school? I grunted. "Will you go away if I tell you?"

Rachel pursed her lips. "Mmm, maybe."

I sat up, scooted back to lean against the headboard, and folded my arms over my chest. "We kissed in her room, her best friend came in, who actually happens to be Tony Mitchell, and he told her some fucking shit about me just trying to get in her pants."

"You and Tony are friends. Why would he do that?"

"Because he realized he didn't want to give her up to me."

"And Lisa believed what he said?" Eyes wider than a car's headlights, Rachel gaped at me. But then her brows furrowed. "Well, of course she would. That's just what you're known for."

"Yeah, rub it in, sis."

"What? Name one girl that you kissed or went out with because you were in love with her."

We stared into each other's eyes for a long moment. Then I said, "Lisa."

Searching my face like she didn't know whether I was kidding or serious, she was silent for a minute. Finally she rolled her eyes. "Oh, the irony of it." Taking off the claw that held her long hair up at the back of her head, she flung herself next to me and leaned her head on my shoulder. "Little Ryan Hunter falls in love for the first time, and that's when he gets payback for all the hearts he's fucked with."

It was strange to hear my sister swearing. I tilted my head, narrowing my eyes, but all I got to see was the top of her head. "Let Mom hear you talking like that and she'll wash your mouth out with soap," I told her. In fact, my mother had done that to me when I was ten. It didn't make me stop using those words, but I sure as hell never said them in front of her again.

Rachel only laughed. "So, what are you going to do about Lisa?"

"What *can* I do? She told me she never wanted to see me again," I muttered dryly.

"And..."

"And nothing. Heck, she threw me out of her room. It's over." Before it had even begun. "I guess she'll forgive Tony for whatever *he* screwed up and be happy with him for...forever."

"She's in love with him?"

"Always has been."

"That's bad. I was totally sure that she was head over heels for you last night."

The sad thing was, for a few hours, I had believed that, too. "Does it mean anything if a girl writes about you in her diary?" I mumbled.

"She mentioned you in there?"

"Mm-hm."

"And she let you read it?" Rachel's voice rose half an octave as she turned her head to stare at me.

"Not exactly."

"You read it secretly?!"

"Could you stop shrieking at me?" I paused then continued with a mumble, "And yes, I did. Not much. Just a few lines. She wrote that she liked how I smelled."

Rachel sat up and looked at me like I'd told her that Santa was going to quit his job and start a new life together with the Easter bunny. "Oh. My. God."

"What?"

"She's totally in love with you."

Was she? Well, she had a strange way of telling me so last night. "She's in love with Mitchell," I grumbled.

"A girl can love more than one guy." Rachel waved a dismissive hand. "And if she noticed how you smell and *liked* it, it's always the most powerful sign that you're the right one for her. A girl can't be with someone she can't smell. That's hormone–ically impossible."

"Hormonically?" I repeated with a dry chuckle.

"Yeah. That's how we tick. She loves your scent, she loves you."

"Great."

"It *is* great. Now where's your phone?"

"Why?"

"Because you're going to call her, apologize for whatever you messed up, and tell her you want to see her again. Duh."

Yeah, right. I forgot that was the most natural thing in the world...

After a moment, Rachel frowned. "You're not going to call her, are you?"

"I don't see a point. Lisa was quite forthright last night."

"Girls don't always mean what they say," she whined.

"You said I was the most annoying little brother one could ever have."

"I meant that."

I quirked my brows at her but didn't reply. With a resigning sigh, my sister rose from the bed and crossed to the door, but before she left me to myself, she turned around once more and said, "Ryan, you're my brother, and I love you. But you are an idiot. And if you don't get over yourself and call that girl who seems to really like you, for Christ's sake, you might be destroying something good. Keep the cake." The door closed silently after her.

I did not call Lisa that day.

From the moment I'd glimpsed a chance for us, I'd tried to do everything right with her. If she didn't see that, it was her fault, not mine. And if she really liked me, as Rachel said, and wanted to talk things out, she should be the one calling, not me!

That night, I fell in and out of sleep in thirty-minute intervals. And every time I woke up, the first thing I did was check my phone for new texts. The only messages that came in were from Justin. He was concerned because I'd ignored his calls all day. Not bothering to answer him or to check my cell for texts any longer, I turned my phone off close to midnight. But I didn't sleep any better after that.

Thursday was the first time in my life that I missed soccer practice for a reason other than a broken ankle. I just couldn't be bothered to look at Mitchell's face. Winter called me afterward and let me know that everyone got the story of the botched evening from Tony today. Only Tony made me look like an asshole who'd hassled Lisa. Alex wanted to know what had happened after Mitchell had left us alone. I didn't care to give deets to anyone. Bad enough that Rachel had coaxed so much information out of me for a piece of cake that my mother had carried away in the morning, untouched.

"She's not interested in me," I told Alex and made clear I wasn't going to say more on that matter.

When Justin called me a little later for the seventh time in two days, I finally answered his call, too. "Hey," I said.

"Why do I have to fucking hear from my little brother what happened to my best friend?"

Someone was pissed, all right. "Sorry, dude. I wasn't in the mood for big conversations."

In the little pause Justin made, he abandoned his anger completely and adopted a compassionate tone. "She rebuffed you?"

"Rebuffed?" I laughed bitterly. "She kicked me to hell."

"Oh crap. How are you doing?"

"I'm a useless shit these days," I confessed.

"I can hear that. Want me to come over and hang out?"

"No," I drawled.

"Wanna go down to the arcade and play some foosball? Get your mind off the girl?"

"Nah, I don't want to do anything really. I'll just watch some TV, maybe get hearing loss from Nickleback." Or stare at the ceiling for another night.

"Okay. Give me a shout if you need anything, dude."

"Yeah, thanks." I hung up and tossed my phone onto the comforter.

Raking a hand through my hair, I dropped into my desk chair, spinning so that I could gaze out the window. That was all I did the entire week. It was either the window, the blank wall, or the ceiling. And whichever was currently on the program, I always saw a heart-shaped face with pretty apple-green eyes smiling back at me.

Maybe Rachel was right. Maybe I was about to destroy something really good and meaningful. But even if I got back on my feet to fight for Lisa again, how could I ever compete against *angelic* Tony?

It was a message from Justin on Saturday that made me change my mind.

I JUST HEARD FROM NICK, WHO HEARD IT FROM ALEX WINTER, WHO HEARD IT FROM MITCHELL HIMSELF, THAT LISA TURNED MITCHELL DOWN THIS

MORNING.

Staring at this message for over thirty minutes, I wondered what Tony had tried with Lisa and how the story had managed to work a circuit. But what did I care as long as the outcome was the same? If Mitchell failed, maybe I had a chance after all...

With my thumb hovering over Lisa's name on the display, I battled my heart back into place. Calling her suddenly seemed like the right thing to do. Trying to get things straight between us. I'd do as Rachel had suggested and apologize. I'd make Lisa understand that I wasn't fooling around with her—that I loved her.

I wiped my thumb over the call button and waited for the line to connect. It rang once, twice. *God, please let her answer.* Three times. Four. My hope turned into fear then frustration. Five. Six. The call went to voice mail. Fuck.

A small part of me hoped this wasn't her evading my call on purpose but that she just didn't have her phone with her right then and would answer later, when she got back. It was also that small part of me that made me call her a couple more times that day. With the same result—only to reach her voice mail again.

Before I went to bed that night, I decided to give it one last try with a text message. PLEASE TALK TO ME.

Nothing came back...right away. But at three o'clock in the morning, my cell went off on vibrate on my nightstand, ripping me out of a light sleep. A text had come in, and it was from Lisa. My heart lurched to my throat as I opened it. Hopefully she had forgiven me. Heck, she must have. A text in the middle of the night could only mean that one thing.

Or could it?

There were three words on the display. Words that stopped my heart for a couple of seconds and that made me want to break everything in my room.

GO TO HELL.

CHAPTER 13

ON TUESDAY, I went to soccer practice in the afternoon. Everyone stared at me. And this wasn't me being paranoid. They stared so blatantly that it hurt. Lacing my cleats gave me a moment where I could ignore them, but when it was time to set up teams for a scrimmage, I faced a crowd that screamed for answers. Their quizzical glares and their mumbling behind cupped hands got on my nerves fast.

"All right," I growled after I had named Winter captain of the opposite team and had picked Frederickson, Torres, and Miller to play with me. "You wanna know what happened? I was out with Matthews, it was a nice evening, but apparently we're not made for each other. Period. Can we please play soccer now?"

"What did you do to her that she left the team?" Audrey Hollister demanded with furrowed brows. "Did you...I mean, were you two—"

"Of course not," Mitchell snarled before Audrey could finish her question. He cast an annihilating scowl in my direction. "Liz would never sleep with *him*. He fucking kissed her is all."

I turned to face him fully. "That's a lot more than you ever worked up the nerve to do with her."

"That's because she's my friend, and I respect her." Mitchell strode forward until we glared at each other from a foot away. "I'm not desperate to get every girl in town into my bed."

The dipshit hit a nerve that clenched the muscles in my gut. "Oh, but *I* am, right?" I sucker-punched his shoulders, making him stumble back a few steps.

Tony steadied fast and returned the shove. "Lisa is the only one you could never have, and that's driving you crazy."

"She'd be with me now if you hadn't spouted that bullshit about me playing with her!"

"Lisa is way beyond your level. She would never choose you." He cast me a scornful look. "Because she doesn't hang out with rats."

The next thing I knew we were on the ground fighting for a truth that we both knew and that no one else needed to hear. I took a hard punch to my ribs, but I gave Mitchell a black eye in turn. Alex and Frederickson dragged me off of Tony before he turned blue in my headlock.

"Dudes, get a grip!" Alex shouted at us. "You're on the same team, whether or not you like it right now. No fighting a teammate."

I tried to battle myself free from his and Frederickson's holds, but they only fastened onto my arms harder, twisting them behind my back.

"I said *no fighting*, Hunter!" Alex snarled next to my ear.

"Take it out in the game, if you must. But if you want to stay captain, you better get a hold of yourself and act like one."

Sending him a killer glare over my shoulder, I wrested my hands free and tromped to the bench, getting rid of my jersey which Mitchell had torn in the fight. He'd destroyed a lot for me lately.

"A to M play with Winter. The rest comes to my team," I told them in a resolute voice as I walked back. That way, I made sure Mitchell ended up on Winter's team, but I also lost Frederickson as our goalie.

Then we played soccer. And it was a bloody game, literally. Whenever Tony and I encountered each other on the field as we went for the ball, somebody had to drag us apart. Alex called the game and practice off early, declaring that he'd had enough of watching us bashing our heads in. Fine with me. I'd have rather stared at the ceiling all day than been around Mitchell one more second.

Back home, I thought about what Alex had said. About the duties of a soccer captain. Maybe I needed to take a break from playing all together. But then I decided I wouldn't let Mitchell take this last important thing from me, too. He'd already taken enough.

I went back to training on Thursday but made it a point not to get into Tony's path anymore. I was done with him. Friends—we *had* been. From the guys, I heard that he wasn't back on good terms with Lisa yet, and I wondered if she'd sent him the same text she'd sent me.

Go to hell.

Every thought I had of Lisa ended with that particular line. Just why did she have to throw me out of her life so irrevocably? A small chance to talk things out...was that really asking too much?

Two weeks went by in which I found a way back to a normal rhythm in my life, but it was more set on autopilot than anything else. Training wasn't fun, but it was okay. At least it distracted me from my aching heart for a few hours each week. The fights with Mitchell had stopped completely, but so had all conversation. That stubborn, selfish bastard. He'd do well to stay out of my way, too.

It was when I noticed him checking his phone for texts or missed calls every ten minutes during practice one day that I realized he was probably hurting just as badly as I was. Even if he hadn't realized it when all of us did, he'd loved the girl from the beginning. And in all that crap with Chloe, he'd lost something very special.

I hadn't seen Tony and Chloe talk to each other even once after that night. In fact, they didn't even look at each other if there was no pressing need. I got the feeling that Tony really hated her, and himself even more for what he'd done. Why Chloe was being so hateful escaped me, though. She'd never made such a clean cut with her former *possessions*—or with anyone who came after Tony. And there were quite a few of my teammates on her list. Luckily, the guys weren't in love with her but just enjoyed a meaningless fling, or else there would have been no more talking at all on the team.

Sometimes I wondered if Chloe raced through the guys just to hurt Tony. And sometimes I wondered why Tony didn't give a damn. Maybe he hadn't been in love with Chloe after all and just needed that one-nighter to find out.

Ah, what did I care? He lived his life now, and I lived mine. Just like Lisa lived her life without the two of us.

What a crappy development...

Walking up next to Tony to get my things, I wondered how much of the friendship he and I had shared I really was missing. I hadn't played *Call of Duty* in ages, and there was still a monster supply of cheese crackers in a drawer in my room.

With his back to me, Tony pocketed his phone and dragged out a sigh that he certainly thought no one would hear. I stuffed my cleats into my backpack and zipped it closed as I said, "We both lost her."

Tony spun around, no doubt shocked about the fact that I'd spoken to him—in a normal voice and not roaring like a mad lion. But his stunned expression quickly turned into a dry look. "Right. And you're telling me this, why?"

I shrugged one shoulder. "I just think there's no point in hating you, when she won't pick either one of us in the end."

Tony just stared at me for a second, and though he said nothing, I was sure that he was chewing my words over. He'd have lots of time for that because I turned on the spot and headed for my car.

I wasn't any happier that day, but it felt good to finally let go of my wrath. Hating Tony after half a life of friendship was an exhausting thing, and nothing I wanted to keep up any longer. What he made of it was his problem.

Some time that evening, my phone went off in my jeans pocket, and when I fished it out, his name showed on the display. It was a text. I turned the volume of my music down and flung myself onto my bed to read what he'd come up with after half a day of mulling. Hopefully he'd invited himself over for a round of *CoD* because, hands down, Justin had no idea how to play cool video games.

But the text Mitchell actually sent me struck me dumb for a total of ten minutes.

REMEMBER WHERE WE CAUGHT LIZARDS AND NUMBED THEM WITH YOUR DAD'S MEDS? I'M HERE WITH A GIRL THAT CAN'T WAIT TO SEE YOU AGAIN, BUT SHE'S TOO STUBBORN TO TELL YOU SO. JUST THOUGHT YOU SHOULD KNOW.

The place he described was a small pond in the woods. And the girl he meant was...mine. As the information sank in, it took me a few moments to restart my heart, but then it shot into high speed and it was all I heard drumming in my ears.

Lisa wanted to see me? I wasn't banned to hell any longer, so why was I still sitting on my bed and staring at that message? I stripped off my tee and buttoned my favorite black shirt, rolling the sleeves up to my elbows. Then I ran some gel through my hair and turned it into what I hoped was an irresistible chaos.

A grin started to grow on my lips as I raced my car down the street, which spread wider the closer I got to the woods. Leaving the car parked at the dead end, I hiked the final half mile. Voices drifted to me, and soon I glimpsed two bikes leaning against a tree. In just a few seconds I would see her again.

Holy shit, I was actually getting nervous.

And then she was there, sitting on a log with her back to me. Her long, beautiful hair cascaded down her shoulders. My heart wanted to give out, but at least I could make my legs work.

I had no idea what they were talking about when she asked Tony, who sat mirroring her on that log, "Maybe. Who's coming?"

"Andy, Sasha, Alex," he replied, not looking away from her, though he must have noticed me coming. "He's with Simone now, by the way. Frederickson will come if he doesn't have to sit his baby brother—"

At that point it was clear to me that he was talking about the movie night in two days that I'd let Alex talk me into. I didn't know that someone had invited Tony, too. But it was good to know.

"And then of course—him." Tony nodded in my direction.

Lisa jerked her head around so fast, it must have hurt in her neck. Her eyes were huge, and her sweet mouth hung slightly open. Kissable lips were the first thought that came to my mind as we stared at each other. Then I realized I should actually say something. "Am I disrupting anything?"

Tony rose from the makeshift bench. "Nope. I was just about to leave."

Startled even more, Lisa cut him a glance and then hissed, "What are you doing?"

She didn't know about the text. That much I'd figured out. Leaning down to her ear, Tony whispered something back that I didn't hear, but when he straightened again, he told her in a normal voice, "See you later."

His gaze skated to me, too, as he said it, and I gave a subtle nod when he walked past me.

Lisa's eyes were the only part of her currently moving. She still had her legs hugged to her chest and her back to me, and I noticed her hitched breathing. Maybe it was mean of us to surprise her like that, but it felt so awfully good to see her again. And that she didn't run away, or shout at me to do so, was definitely a good sign.

I lifted one leg across the tree trunk and settled down behind her, looping my arms around her beguiling body and pulling her back against my chest. It didn't matter that she went stiff like a board, she felt wonderful in my arms. "I'm sorry for what happened, but I never meant to hurt you," I said softly, nuzzling her neck. "And I certainly didn't have any bad intentions. I swear."

Slowly, her body relaxed against mine. "Yeah, I guess I know that," she drawled. "Susan told me a few interesting things today."

I caught my breath. "Did she?" Heck, what had the book lover told her? Probably everything about my fight with Tony, and then some. But what was I afraid of? Lisa had a right to know. And if it made her forgive me, like she seemed to have done, I would have to thank Miller the next time I saw her.

I hugged Lisa a little tighter, pressing my cheek against her brow. "So, what are we going to make of this situation?"

"*Situation?* What do you mean?"

What did I mean? Oh, I could be quite creative with my dream girl in my arms. "I mean you...me..." I kissed her shoulder to give her an idea of what I meant. "Alone...in this place..."

Her skin was coated with a nice layer of goose bumps when I trailed my tongue in a slim spiral toward her neck and up the column of her throat. "With only the frogs to watch us..." I finished with pressing a gentle kiss on the tempting spot behind her ear.

Lisa didn't move, and I hated not to see the reaction to my caresses in her eyes. Shaping my palm against her burning cheek, I tilted her face slowly toward me. "What do you say, Matthews? Should we give it a try?"

Lisa remained silent long enough to make me feel uncomfortable and lose all hope. But then a reluctant smile curved her lips. "Only if you start using my first name, *Hunter.*"

The relief and joy I felt made me laugh. And also how she called me Hunter. When she said my name, it always sounded like something dangerous. And hell, with those tender lips in front of me, it was too easy to turn into a wild wolf with her. I brushed her cheekbone with the tip of my nose, then I stole the first sweet kiss after three torturous weeks.

But before I went on with something I knew I wouldn't be able to stop later, there was something I needed to sort out first. "While we're at it, *Lisa*...I have a condition, too."

"You do?" She quirked her eyebrows. "What is it?"

"For the time being," I said very slowly, so she would know how serious I was, "I'll be the only one climbing through your window."

A beautiful laugh escaped her and made my heart skip inside my chest. "I think I can agree to that."

"You *think*?" That wasn't enough for me by far. Gently biting into her bottom lip, I wanted to coax out a real promise.

Lisa pulled back, smiling. "Okay, you win. You'll be the only one."

That was all I needed to hear. I stroked her silky hair from her forehead and made her look directly into my eyes. "See, baby, that sounds a damn lot better."

And the next thing I knew our tongues were entangled in a kiss that raised the temperature around us by at least ten degrees. I made her turn around on that log so she would straddle my legs and I could run my hands over the length of her amazing body. She shivered when I touched her and released a moan that drove me wild.

Leaning back on the fallen tree with my feet still planted

on the ground on either side, I pulled Lisa down with me, just to feel every bit of her body on top of mine. We kissed until our lips were swollen and an owl hooted deeper in the wood, reminding me that it was way past time to take Lisa home.

"It's quite late. Do you want me to drive you?" I asked as we walked back to my car, our fingers laced and me wheeling her mountain bike with the other hand. "We can come back for your bike tomorrow."

"Nah, I'm not scared of the dark. And it's not far, anyway."

I didn't like the idea of Lisa riding home alone in the dead of night, but neither did I want to force her into anything. "All right. Will you send me a message when you're home? Just so I know I don't have to go looking for you?" When I winked at her, she cracked a smile, and it brightened the dark for me.

The first quarter of a mile, I drove slowly beside her, with my window open, but as we reached the town, our ways parted and I blew her a kiss before I turned left and she kept straight.

Driving up the street to my house, I slowed the car. But I never stopped. I just didn't want to wait half a night before I could see her again. And I sure wouldn't wait for a message to tell me that she'd arrived home safely when I could assure myself of it.

I spun the Audi in the middle of the street, heading back the way I'd come. Three minutes later, I zoomed up the avenue to Lisa's house. As I slammed on the breaks, parking it smoothly next to the curb, she just got off her bike and wheeled it into the shed.

Leaving the headlights on to break through the dark, I got out and followed her into the garden. As she returned from the shed, she walked up to me until her body was flush against mine and wrapped her arms around my neck. "What did you forget this time?" she teased me.

"Same as always," I answered and took her mouth in a savagely slow and tender good-night kiss.

CHAPTER 14

LISA SMELLED FANTASTIC. We'd spent most of Sunday at my parents' beach house, hanging out in the sun, fooling around in the sea, or kissing in my bed. She was wearing this hot, green, triangle bikini top and shorts as she lay on top of me right now, arms folded under her chin on my chest, gazing into my eyes.

Playing with the silky strands of her hair, I wished I could freeze time and never let her out of this room again.

"What are you thinking about?" she demanded, tilting her head a little.

"That I can't believe how I'm finally able to hold you."

Lisa seemed to like my answer, because she dragged herself farther up then and placed a soft kiss on my lips. I totally started getting into that again, but when I stroked her cheek, she caught my wrist and glanced at my watch. "It's past five," she said. "We have to go back now if we don't want to be late."

"I'm fine with being late," I told her before I thrust my hand in her hair and made her kiss me again.

Her body shook on my chest as she laughed. "Stop it, Hunter." Then she got off of me, leaving my bare chest

ANNA KATMORE

yearning for her warmth. She closed the window, which she'd insisted we keep open the entire time. Initially, she'd told me she just wanted to smell the sea breeze, but I was pretty sure it had to do with a possible escape if one of my folks showed up here unexpectedly.

When she stood in the doorway, hands on her hips and arching one brow at me, it was clear that she wasn't coming back, so I got up, too, and picked up my shirt from the floor, which I'd discarded over an hour ago. Closing the buttons, I watched Lisa slip on her red blouse and regretted I hadn't hid the piece earlier, when I'd had time to. I liked looking at her when she was wearing as little as possible. Her bikini would totally do.

Outside, I locked the door and dropped the keys back into the potted plant on the porch. But I couldn't resist hooking my fingers through the belt loops of Lisa's short jeans and pulling her into me one last time before we started to walk back. "Come here, sexy wench," I growled, and unbuttoned the top of her blouse.

"What are you doing? We just left your room." Playfully, she slapped my hands away. "I think I have enough hickeys all over me for a day or two."

Ah, I wasn't sure about that. There was definitely a spot on her left shoulder begging for another.

"It's hot," I teased. "And you look amazing in that bikini. I can't allow you to hide that from me." I nibbled a path down her neck, getting closer to the spot on her shoulder that I wanted to mark next.

The shivers running along her skin were proof that she loved what I was doing to her, even if she tried to fend me off. "If you don't stop that, we'll be late for the movie."

"What do I care about a movie, when I have my lovely girlfriend all to myself?"

"Tony and the others are waiting."

The mention of that name made me stop. Tony and I had yet to talk things out between us, and I didn't like Lisa thinking about him when she was with me. But I knew they had a history going way back, and Tony would always be part of our relationship, because she would never give him up as a good friend. I told myself I could handle this. But right now, I'd rather not hear that name when I was nibbling my girlfriend.

I quickly glanced at my watch. Five twenty. "We still have an hour and a half."

"I want to shower before we go out."

"All right. But this—" I slid the blouse down her arms and cast her a determined grin. "Is mine." A short, hard kiss was enough to stop her protest.

Lacing my fingers through hers, I dragged her down the stairs after me, and we ambled back to where I had parked my car. The cool sea brushed around our ankles. I tucked Lisa's blouse partly into my back pocket then bent down to roll up the hems of my jeans.

As I straightened, I caught Lisa ogling my backside, but she tried to hide her interest and quickly looked away. Her cheeks turned a lovely pink.

"What, Matthews? You like my butt?" I mocked her.

When she looked at me again, she lifted her chin. "Yep. That and a few other things."

"So? What would that be?"

She didn't answer that but scolded me for something I just couldn't stop myself from doing. "Didn't we agree you'd use my first name from now on?"

Innocently, I cocked one brow. "Did we?"

"I think it was one of the conditions, yeah."

"Ah, conditions, conditions," I growled through half a laugh and pulled her closer. "I should have made you swear never to wear anything other than that bikini top when you're with me."

Lisa leaned slightly back and gave me an evil look. "I doubt that's a good idea. Especially when we're at your place. You had me sweating bullets back there."

So I was right about the window. Brushing a strand of hair out of her face, I hooked it behind her ear. "Aw, look who's still worried."

"That is your fault. You scared the crap out of me last time when your mom came in."

"I know. I felt your heart pounding like it would jump out of your chest when I had you pinned to the floor behind the couch." Pursing my lips, I angled my head, looking at her sideways. "Or could it be that you were just excited to be so close to me?" Which was my guess from the start.

Lisa stuck her sweet tongue out at me. "You'll never find out."

Oh, I would find out, if it meant I had to tickle her sexy body until she could breathe no more. Later...

With my arm around her warm shoulders, we walked along the beach, and I thought some more about her fear of someone walking in on us. Finally, I made a decision, one that was totally unusual for me. "I met your parents this morning. I think it's time for you to meet mine," I told her.

Lisa looked appalled. "What, *now*?"

Actually, why not? "There's still plenty of time until the movie begins. And they should both be home right now. We could just pop in for a moment before meeting up with the others."

"But you haven't even told them about me yet."

"So what? You didn't tell yours before you dragged me into your kitchen to say hello." Holy crap, that had been quite an experience. I'd never before been introduced as somebody's boyfriend. But when I glimpsed her mother's delighted face, I relaxed and realized I actually happened to like it quite a bit. Bethany Matthews had kept her promise and never told Lisa we'd met that night three weeks ago. When she'd offered me a delicious-smelling muffin, I winked at her, and she gave me a smile that made me feel totally welcome in her house.

"But you're always cool with everything," Lisa whined now. "I knew it wouldn't trouble you."

"And meeting my parents would be a problem for you?" I

didn't understand her fear. Mom and Dad would love her. Rachel already did.

"You haven't even told me their names."

I didn't see how that was important, so I chuckled. "Their names are Mom and Dad."

Lisa rolled her eyes as her voice took on a sarcastic edge. "Amazing...that's what I call my parents, too."

"Yeah, popular names." I dropped my hand from her shoulders to hug her waist tighter against my hip. Her skin was smooth and warm everywhere and tempted me to stroke her in small circles with my fingertips. "But maybe it isn't such a good idea to meet them now," I added. "They'll make us stay all evening, and we won't be able to get to the show in time."

Instead, I pulled my phone out of my chest pocket.

"Calling someone?" she wanted to know.

I nodded and motioned with one finger on my lips for her to be silent for a moment while I waited for my mother to answer.

"Hello?" Mom sounded breathless, like she had run through the house to get to the phone.

"Mom? Hi."

"Ryan, what's up?"

"Just wanted to say we're going to have a guest for dinner tomorrow."

"Oh. That's nice."

Not only my mom sounded surprised at that announcement, but Lisa's chin also dropped to her chest.

Then my mother added in a teasing tone, "Could it actually be a girl?"

"Yes, a friend," I told her, struggling to sound nonchalant. But with everything Rachel had dragged out of me the other day and surely passed on to my mom, I wasn't fooling anybody. Heck, why did I even try? "Oh, and could you please invite Rach and Phil, too?"

Lisa looked shocked at that news, definitely thinking about decapitating me later.

But what really made me laugh then was Jezebel Hunter's jumping to conclusions. "Rachel and Philip, too? Good lord, Ryan. You aren't getting us all together to tell us I'm going to be a gran come next spring?"

Instantly, my gaze dropped to Lisa's sexy stomach. I had to turn around to make myself look away and stop thinking about how badly I wanted to tickle her bellybutton with my tongue.

"No, Mom," I said into the phone. "If it was that, I swear I wouldn't be calling."

"Thank goodness." My mother released a deep breath. "All right, I'll call Rachel and invite her over. See you later, darling."

After I said goodbye and rang off, I turned back to Lisa and slid a knuckle under her chin, closing her mouth. "We have a date tomorrow evening."

"Yeah, I heard that," she sighed. "So you're going to throw me in there like a bone in front of a wolf pack?"

Ah, this girl was so sweet when she was scared. "Don't

worry. I'll be with you, and I'll protect you all evening. No one gets to gnaw on you." Leaning closer, I nibbled her earlobe then whispered, "Apart from me, that is."

But that didn't convince her that it would be okay, and she whined, "If you liked me one bit, you wouldn't do that."

"I like you two bits, and that's exactly why we need to do this. Now stop worrying. It can't be worse than your father asking me if I knew how to use a condom."

With a gasp, she pulled back. "He asked you that?"

Yeah, I had been as shocked as she was now. But on another note it was funny, too. "Not exactly. He mentioned something like it to your mother when we were out of the room. Didn't you hear him whispering?"

"Oh my *God*, how embarrassing is that?"

For her? Not at all. For me? I'd felt like a bloody beginner.

"Calm down," I told her then. "Your parents are great. And your mom's blueberry muffins are amazing." I kissed her brow and pulled her on, smiling to myself about what was at the tip of my tongue. "But maybe you should assure your dad that I do know how to not knock you up."

Lisa reacted with a blush to my smirk.

As we arrived at the Audi, she turned to me. "Can I have my shirt back now, or do you want me to ride half-naked in your car?"

Man, she shouldn't tempt me like that. "You mean I have a choice?"

"No!" She swatted my arm then reached around me to fish

for her blouse. Her eyes narrowed all of a sudden. "Where is it?"

What, the blouse? I reached back myself and found my pocket empty. We both pivoted and stared down the way we'd come. Oh fucking crap. The red bundle floated on the water, getting washed up and down the beach with a wave.

Lisa dashed for it, but as she held it up against the sun, it was clear I'd get my way and she'd be riding home half-naked.

"Oh, great."

"It's not the end of the world, Lisa," I told her as I walked up to her, laughing about her sweetly scrunched face. Then I took pity on her and unbuttoned my shirt. "You can take mine for the ride home."

Lisa took a minute to gawk at my bare chest again, and it made me feel unspeakably good. But I also couldn't resist mocking her and arched one eyebrow. "Okay. If you don't want it..."

Before I could slip the shirt on again, she jerked it out of my hands, flung it around her shoulders, then shoved her arms through the short sleeves.

She looked hot in my shirt, even though it was way too long for her and covered her hot pants completely. Or maybe it was just because of that...

"I like you in my clothes," I said and pulled her against me, hardly able to suppress an animalistic growl. "You're way too sexy for your own good, Matthews."

I kissed her deeply, satisfying the need to touch her, which stayed with me the entire day. Giving her bottom lip a gentle nip, I eased back. Apparently, my girl wasn't done kissing me, though, because she threaded her fingers in my hair and held me in place, not intending to let me get away from her just yet. Fine with me. I yanked her hard against me, giving her a kiss she could live on through the rest of the evening.

After a couple of minutes, I pulled back and reminded her, "You know we have to get you home so you can shower. And if I remember it right, we're supposed to watch a movie."

Gazing at me with dreamy eyes, she stroked my whiskered cheek. "What do I care about a movie, if I have my gorgeous boyfriend all to myself?"

She was making me eat my own words? That little witch. "Yeah, right. And afterward you'll make me pay for making us late. No way. Get your butt into my car, Matthews. *Now.*"

With a pout, she relented.

We put our shoes on, which we'd left behind in the car, then I drove us to her house. Lisa made me wait by the door until she'd inspected the hallway and made sure that her folks weren't around. Obviously, she didn't like me walking in front of them half-naked. Me neither.

She ushered me past the empty kitchen, but when we headed for the stairs, Mr. Matthews came out of the living room and stopped dead in the threshold. He gave me a once-over, his brows furrowing into a deep V.

"Wet blouse," I said quickly and held out the dirty bundle in my defense. "She needed something to wear."

A laughing Bethany walked up behind her husband and rubbed his upper arm. "I told you he's a gentleman, darling."

Without wasting another moment, Lisa dragged me up to her room. While she rushed through a shower and dressed, I lounged on her bed, this time resisting the urge to read more of her diary. I wanted to be a nice boyfriend. Someone she could rely on and utterly trust.

While she skimmed through the many hoodies in her wardrobe, trying to select one that fit her pink strappy top, I walked up behind her, looped my arms around her middle and rested my chin on her shoulder. "Do you still have the Mickey Mouse hoodie?"

Lisa sent me a startled sideways glance. "The dark gray one?"

"Mm-hm."

"I haven't worn it for over a year."

"I know," I drawled, letting her hear how that fact had bothered me all of last school year. She looked amazing in that sweatshirt, and right now I wanted to give her a choice between either that or the green bikini top again.

Fishing the sweatshirt out from under a stack of other clothes, she mumbled, "I can't believe you still remember this thing."

She had no freaking idea what other memories I'd saved of her over the years. When she pulled the snugly fitting sweatshirt on and turned in my arms, I nearly asked her to do her hair in those sexy pigtails again, which she'd last done when she wore this outfit. But I decided to keep that option for a day when I wouldn't have to share her with anyone else.

Fifteen minutes later, we climbed out of my car in front of the theater. While Lisa headed over to Frederickson and Alex— the guy had finally grabbed the girl he wanted as well—I joined Andy and Sasha by the counter and paid for two tickets.

Walking back to the others, I found Lisa standing way too close to Tony, who must have arrived just a minute ago. The sight of the two of them clenched my gut. Lisa had told me that he'd kissed her before sending me the text on Friday night, but that she'd felt nothing for him. I believed her, but there was this small part of me that felt insecure nonetheless.

I hooked two fingers into the waistband of her jeans and pulled her just a small step back, marking territories here. Lisa reached for my hand, squeezing it with the utmost trust and confidence. With it, she coaxed out my relieved sigh.

Then I turned to Tony. "Hey, Mitchell. Are we cool?" I held out a fist to him.

He bumped it without hesitation. "Of course."

And that was the moment when everything slipped into place. I had my friend back, and the most beautiful girl—the only one I'd ever wanted—stood by my side and laced her fingers through mine.

When it was time to get to our seats and everyone got moving, I held Lisa back for another moment.

"What's wrong?" she demanded, tilting her head.

"What did Mitchell say to you?" I just had to know to be

Ryan Hunter   217 able to check the matter off and completely relax with my girlfriend.

"He asked me if I was happy."

I leaned down and touched my forehead to hers, needing to know only one more thing. "Are you?"

Lisa lifted to her toes and placed a sweet little kiss on my cheek. "Absolutely."

EPILOGUE

"AW, PLEASE, CAN'T we just go back to my house and make out there for the rest of the evening?"

I laughed at Lisa's whiny face, and even though that option was one helluva temptation, I dragged her through the front door with me. Standing in the foyer of my house, I wondered who'd be the first to come and meet my girlfriend. Rachel or Mom?

As it turned out, they walked out of the dining room together, both struggling to keep their beaming expressions under control. I helped Lisa out of my leather jacket, which she'd demanded as a paycheck for this official meeting, and hung it on the coatrack while Jezebel Hunter introduced herself.

"Please, call me Jessie, dear," my mother offered when Lisa shook her hand and told *Mrs. Hunter* what a nice house she had. Mom never liked being called by her last name, no matter who it was. Jeez, a day at my school—with my friends—would actually kill her.

I stepped to Lisa's side and took her hand, totally to the delight of my big sister. "Lisa—you already met my mom and sister. Mom—this is Lisa Matthews." I took a deep breath. "My girlfriend."

Rachel kept a straight face at that, but I saw how her hand fisted at her side for a possible victory punch in the air. We grinned at each other, then the Hunter women ushered me and Lisa into the dining room, where Dad had just finished setting the table.

Lisa waved *hi* at Phil by the window, then she shook hands with my dad. We sat through a cool dinner with my folks, and even though Lisa seemed a little stiffer than usual, she obviously enjoyed the time with my family. She and Dad soon found out that they had actually met before. A very long time ago.

"I must have been four years old, if that," Lisa said to me, "when your dad told me that I couldn't take my fish with me into the tub. Yeah, somebody should have told me *before* I played *Free Willy* and gave them a new home."

We laughed at that, and under the table, I ran my palm up and down her thigh to give her a feeling of comfort. She placed her hand on mine and squeezed.

After dinner, I managed to tear Lisa away from my family, who had adopted her the first moment she'd walked through our door, and kidnapped her into the garden. Down by the gazebo, there was still Rachel's and my old swing. I sat down on it, grabbing the hem of my leather jacket, which was now Lisa's, and pulled her between my legs.

"Did you know that you drive me completely out of my mind whenever you wear any of my clothes?" I said, looking up at her face.

Lisa gave me one of her tight-lipped smiles that were always a sign that she was touched by what I'd said. "You mentioned something like that yesterday, when I had your shirt on."

"Remind me to send you off with a few of my T-shirts tonight, so you can always wear them when I come to your place."

"Only tees?" She pulled my Indians cap off my head and put it on, threading her ponytail through the back. "How about that?"

Hell, if she wanted me on my knees, she totally had me there. "Girl, you're driving me to my limits of self-control," I growled and pulled her down on my lap, starting to nibble the skin at her throat.

She threw her head back and laughed out loud. "Ryan Hunter, you're insatiable."

"When it comes down to you, Matthews, I totally am."

Lisa wrapped her arms around my neck and looked at me with shiny eyes from the cap's shade. Many things played out in her gaze at that moment. Fascination. Happiness. Even a little devotion.

"I absolutely know what you're thinking right now," I teased her.

"Is that so? Then what am I thinking?"

I licked my lips, trying to look serious when I said, "You're thinking that you can't wait to get up to my room with me and have me strip you naked on my bed."

Her cheeks flushed an adorable pink. "Close, but not quite the truth," she told me with a sweetly sarcastic voice and a dry grin.

I knew how close my taunt had hit home, but she was right. The one thing that was really written in her eyes had nothing to do with carnal needs. This time I didn't have to struggle for a serious face. "You're thinking that you never believed how easily you could forget Anthony Mitchell if you only gave yourself a chance with someone else."

Lisa's eyes grew a bit wider.

"With someone like me," I continued, brushing the back of my knuckles along her jaw. "You're thinking that you've totally misjudged me and that I'm not at all the *impossible* guy"—I rolled my eyes to mimic her—"you always thought me to be."

Her lips parted slightly. One of her hands slipped from my neck and rested softly against my chest. Yeah, I'd stunned her with what I read in her eyes, but I wasn't done yet. "And you're thinking that you might actually be falling for me."

The way she gazed at me now had me wondering if she'd forgotten how to breathe again. I pulled my cap off her head and placed it back on her, reversing it. Then I touched my brow to hers. "Do you want to know what *I* am thinking now?"

She gave a shy nod, her warm breath caressing my skin.

"I think it's time that you know I'm in love with you, Lisa. That you've been my very own sunshine for a very long time. And that I don't intend to let you out of my arms ever again."

It took only a slight tilt of my head to meet her lips with mine. Soft and tender, she felt like my personal little piece of heaven. The taste of her made my head spin. Lisa had developed a certain talent for kissing that always threatened to make me lose control and forget everything around us.

For a moment, our tongues twisted around each other while our lips barely touched. With one hand at the back of her neck, I pressed her toward me a little harder, turning our light kiss into something deep and wicked. Her fingers clawed my shirt, and she pressed herself against me in a way that had me thinking of skin rubbing on skin and what I wanted to do with her after throwing her over my shoulder and carrying her up to my room.

Panting, Lisa pulled away from me, and from only two inches apart, our gazes locked. I wiped my thumb across her swollen bottom lip. "What's wrong, sunshine?"

She took a deep breath, smiling briefly. "You were right with almost everything you said before. But you got one thing wrong."

"What is that?"

Her hand shaped against my cheek, something she always did when she was about to give a little bit more of herself to me. "I'm not falling for you, Ryan Hunter," she said and narrowed her eyes, slowly shaking her head. Then a perfect smile curved her lips. "I'm already in love."

Playlist

Just Give Me A Reason - P!nk ft. Nate Ruess
(Theme song. It has always been her)

Feel Again – OneRepublic
(Skateboarding and meeting friends)

It's Time – Imagine Dragons
(She's going to be on the team)

She Doesn't Mind – Sean Paul
(At Hunter's party)

Stop That Train – Bob Marley & The Wailers
(A special memory of Ryan and Justin)

If I Lose Myself – OneRepublic
(Kiss her...or not?)

Lost Then Found – Leona Lewis ft. OneRepublic
(He's a brokenhearted boy)

Come Home – OneRepublic ft. Sara Bareilles
(A kiss on the swing)

Get a sneak peek into the third book of the
Grover Beach Team series,
T is for...

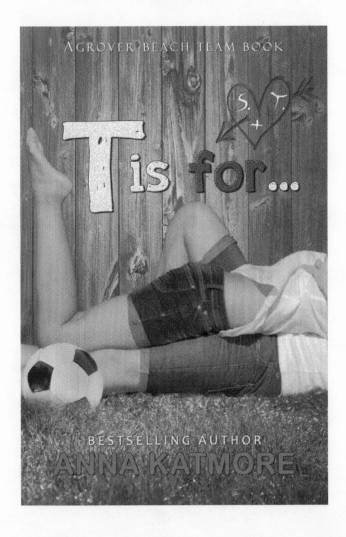

"I don't know what's currently going on in Anthony Mitchell's mind, but you're definitely taking up a lot of space in there."

Life isn't easy for Samantha Summers, daughter of an army general. Moving from one continent to another every other year helps a teenage girl learn 4 different languages in record time. But it's also killing her social life. And when a totally hot guy in her new town gives her hell because she's the cousin of a girl he once dated who then spurned him, the prospect of the coming school year makes Sam want to call it quits.

There's just one thing even more unnerving than all that put together. For some strange reason, she can't seem to stop daydreaming about this impossible guy.

ABOUT THE AUTHOR

ANNA KATMORE prefers blue to green, spring to winter, and writing to almost everything else. It helps her escape from a boring world to something with actual adventure and romance, she says. Even when she's not crafting a new story, you'll see her lounging with a book in some quiet spot. She was 17 when she left Vienna to live in the tranquil countryside of Austria, and from there she loves to plan trips with her family to anywhere in the world. Two of her favorite places? Disneyland and the deep dungeons of her creative mind.

For more information, please visit her website at www.annakatmore.com

36591170R00139

Made in the USA
Lexington, KY
26 October 2014